"I Saw You Kissing My Son!"

"I was not kissing your son," Stevie snapped. "Your son gave me a peck on the cheek." When she noted his unbelieving look, her hazel eyes turned dangerous. "This, Mr. Ward, is what I call a kiss!"

Grasping the lapels of his evening jacket, she leaned against him, bending him backward over his desk. Her mouth slanted over his half-parted lips, effectively smothering his astonishment as her tongue made a quick, intimate taunt.

"Now you know the difference. I don't need to seduce boys, Quintin Ward." With a swish of black lace, she turned and disappeared out the door.

ELAINE RACO CHASE

recently exchanged Schenectady, New York, for the sunny beaches of east coast Florida. Here, with her husband, daughter, and son, she enjoys swimming, teaches creative writing, and reads detective novels. Formerly an advertising copywriter, Elaine writes romantic comedies and believes loving and laughing make wonderful bedfellows.

Dear Reader:

SILHOUETTE DESIRE is an exciting new line of contemporary romances from Silhouette Books. During the past year, many Silhouette readers have written in telling us what other types of stories they'd like to read from Silhouette, and we've kept these comments and suggestions in mind in developing SILHOUETTE DESIRE.

DESIREs feature all of the elements you like to see in a romance, plus a more sensual, provocative story. So if you want to experience all the excitement, passion and joy of falling in love, then SILHOUETTE DESIRE is for you.

I hope you enjoy this book and all the wonderful stories to come from SILHOUETTE DESIRE. I'd appreciate any thoughts you'd like to share with us on new SILHOUETTE DESIRE, and I invite you to write to us at the address below:

Karen Solem
Editor-in-Chief
Silhouette Books
P.O. Box 769
New York, N.Y. 10019

ELAINE RACO CHASE
Calculated Risk

Silhouette Desire
Published by Silhouette Books New York
America's Publisher of Contemporary Romance

SILHOUETTE BOOKS, a Division of Simon & Schuster, Inc.
1230 Avenue of the Americas, New York, N.Y. 10020

Copyright © 1983 by Elaine Raco Chase

Distributed by Pocket Books

ISBN: 0-671-46227-X

First Silhouette Books printing December, 1983

10 9 8 7 6 5 4 3 2 1

America's Publisher of Contemporary Romance

Printed in the U.S.A.

BC91

Calculated Risk

1

Stephanie Brandt?"

Hazel eyes were jarred from their intense involvement with the pages of *Variety* by the yellow hard hat that was slammed on the white linen tablecloth.

"Are you Stephanie Brandt?" grated the forceful masculine voice.

Blinking in surprise, she looked up to confront the man who threatened her with her own name. "Yes."

"I want you to stop seducing my son. Leave him alone, lady; stop all the presents. Stop everything! If you don't, I'll file sexual misconduct charges against you."

The man's rough-hewn face was livid, but his words were coherent, emphatic and loud enough to capture the attention of the other early dinner patrons at Le Châlet. Quickly regaining her composure, Stevie rose to her imposing sixty-eight inches, her voice a low, fierce whisper. "Who the hell are you and what are you talking about?"

"Shut up." The stranger's large hand conquered her black tweed suit-covered shoulder. Strong fingers pressed into her fragile collarbone, effectively forcing Stevie back into the Queen Anne dining chair. "Rob's only seventeen," he growled, "and you're . . . you're thirty-two? Thirty-four? Hell! There's room for a whole other person!"

Stevie was doing a Herculean job of damming her own cresting anger. She was not a screamer or a shrieker, but *no one* ever told her to shut up. Her attempt at twisting her shoulder free was thwarted by the pain this man's powerful grip caused. "Now wait just a minute," she panted from her exertions, "I don't—"

"Shut up, lady!" he snarled again as his hand pressured her agitated figure to remain seated. "All I've heard is 'Stephanie, Stephanie, Stephanie'! When Rob first started talking about you, I thought you were a high school cheerleader." His massive chest heaved under deep breaths. "It just took me a while to put two and two together." Brown eyes narrowed in sneering contemplation. "Is this a quirk with you, lady? Do you get your kicks sexually dominating young boys?"

Her mauve-tinted mouth dropped open. "Hey . . . now . . . you . . ." Stevie's abject denial stuttered into silence under the bruising dark gaze and animal rage that contorted her accuser's features.

"I've talked to a lawyer." A blunt forefinger punctured the air inches from her nose. "I can have you arrested for gross immorality, moral turpitude, contributing to the delinquency of a minor and exploitation of a professional relationship for personal gain."

The dark-haired stranger reached into the breast pocket of his denim work jacket and yanked out a paper. "And don't think I'm sucker enough to pay this!"

Mesmerized, Stevie witnessed the ensuing action unfold as if in slow motion. The green letterhead briefly fluttered like a kite on a current of air before it drifted down to cover her dinner plate. His white-knuckled fist pounded on top of it. The voucher merged with the half-eaten quiche Florentine. The egg-custard-and-spinach filling oozed off the china onto the pristine cloth.

Finally, to her utter relief, the hard hat and its granite owner turned and stalked out of the restaurant, his work boots ringing every step against the polished wood floor.

Rose-tipped fingers pulled at the high collar on her pleated-front blouse. But the tightness that constricted Stevie's throat came more from the whispering patrons and their speculative glances than the magenta silk collar. That trite phrase *wishing to fade into the woodwork* had never held so much meaning.

The tuxedo-clad maître d's jaunty figure bustled

toward her. "Mademoiselle Brandt, I apologize.
That . . . that man said he had an urgent message
for you or I would have never allowed him in."

Bernardo's hands fluttered like dizzy butterflies
over the table. "No suit. No tie. No reservations!"
His black eyebrows bounced in alarm *"Zut!* What is
this!"

Two perfectly manicured male fingers lifted the
grease-stained stationery from the dinner plate.
"That . . . that uncouth brute! Look at my
quiche!"

Stevie winced, noting that Bernardo's cry of pain
fostered another burst of attention toward the tiny
table, which was partially secluded by potted parlor
palms. "The quiche, as always, was magnificent."
Her husky contralto sought to soothe. She took the
letter from his hand, wiped it on her napkin and
made it disappear into her jacket pocket.

"Put the dinner and a generous tip on my
account." She stood and brushed pastry crumbs
off her black wool skirt. "Could you please have
my car brought around, Bernardo?" Stevie smiled
slightly as the restaurateur went away, mumbling
French-fractured English and waving expressive
European hands.

Pride backboned with willpower got Stephanie
Brandt through the dining room. She even managed enough aplomb to enter into a few brief,
meaningless conversations with casual acquaintances. Once outside, her composure was soon
destroyed by the anger she had been too stunned
to express.

By the time the blue Mercedes completed its two-block swing through Music Row, Stephanie Brandt had chanted her mantra a thousand times and turned it into a word Mother had never taught her! Parking the diesel sedan in the space marked Reserved, she grabbed her purse and leather attaché case and bolted from the car, slamming the door with fury.

She inhaled six deep lungfuls of crisp January air and forced herself to assume her usual cool control. "Sorry about that." Her hand patted an apology against the luxury car's handcrafted precision door.

Gloria Lansing looked over the top of her bifocals as her boss walked into the reception area. "That was a quick dinner. I haven't finished these contracts, and—"

Stevie's hand waved her quiet. "Do I know anyone named Ward? Rob or . . . or Rod? Or"—she made an expressive face as she took another look at the crumpled and stained invoice— "how about Quintin Ward? Cedar Lane off Franklin Road?"

Turning off her typewriter, Gloria studied her seething employer with awe. In the two years during which she had been administrative assistant to Stephanie Brandt, nothing and no one had ever evoked this type of reaction. As president of one of Nashville's most prestigious talent management firms, Stevie's name was synonymous with personal discipline and self-control.

Gloria quickly sifted through the massive Rolodex information file. "You know a Carleton Ward in LA, Harry Ward in Queens and Kyle Ward, the backup drummer for the Pursuit of Happiness Singers." She pulled a pencil from the neat gray bun on top of her head and tapped a blank address card. "No Rod, Rob or Quintin Ward."

Hazel eyes narrowed on the paper one last time. "Find out who they are." Stevie tossed the florist bill on the desk. "Pay this and cancel any standing order. It seems the perfect red rose that's been arriving every day for a month is not another thank-you from the Pit Stops for their album going platinum. It's from some seventeen-year-old boy whose father just accused me of seduction!" Her hands made a gesture of disgust.

"Well, well!" Gloria winked saucily. "And I would have bet you preferred a more aged cut of prime beef." The easy way in which she joked with Stephanie came from her status as friend and confidante more than employee.

"Please." The word came out a groan. Stevie prowled the vacant reception area. "There I was, minding my own business, enjoying a leisurely dinner before the concert, when I get" —her hand moved beneath her jacket to massage her sore shoulder—"mangled in public by a man wearing work boots, denim and a T-shirt with an obscene foreign word printed on it. In Le Châlet of all places!" Her fist landed a heavy punch against the desk. "Damn Quintin Ward!" Stevie's eyes glowed more green than amber. "Thank God for potted palms and the fact that this guy had shoulders like a linebacker." Her fingers pushed through thick russet hair, shattering the soft waves that whispered across her shoulders. "I don't think too many people could actually hear and see what was going on," came her relieved murmur.

"What *was* going on?" Gloria demanded, her interest piqued as she stalked her boss's every step.

Stevie gritted her teeth. "He wouldn't let me talk. He kept slinging accusations. He'd push me back in the chair. . . ." Her emotions were swelling out of control. "He had the nerve to say I looked thirty-four and . . . and he kept telling me to shut up!" Again her fist attempted to shatter the oak desk top.

She swallowed hard. "If I could have stood up, I would have decked that man!" Her thumb and forefinger pinched the bridge of her nose, hoping to relieve the mounting pressure. "I'd love to know how he found me at that restaurant."

Gloria, who had been trying to coordinate Stevie's rather disjointed tirade, suddenly shifted in discomfort in the navy posture chair. "Ouch! That's my fault." Noting a pair of speculatively arched tawny brows, she hastily cleared up the mystery. "I got a phone call from a man who claimed to be the florist about another flower delivery. I thought it'd be a little flattering PR to have them bring the rose to you at the restaurant."

An exhausted sigh escaped from Stevie's lips. "That was a nice idea; unfortunately . . ." Weary hands massaged her face. "Gloria, could you please find me some aspirin and send out for a burger." She grimaced. "My dinner is on the florist's bill. And"—her hand twisted the latch on her office door—"find this kid named Ward!"

Stevie traded the reception area's album-art-covered, midnight blue walls and high-impact chrome decor for the decidedly more subdued environment of the president's office. The cinnamon sculptured carpet, butter-cream leather sofa and side chairs complemented the carved oak wall panels.

The oversize executive chair was an instant balm to Stevie's taut nerves. Black pumps were slid off and ankles propped and crossed on the desk corner as her tense body relaxed into the plush leather cushions. Her red-gold hair formed a vibrant cascade around an oval face that held a smattering of freckles expertly hidden under an ivory-tinted makeup base.

Taupe-shadowed eyelids drifted closed as her breathing became more regular and her mood adjusted to the tranquility of her surroundings. A smile curved the corners of her full lips. For most people their work atmosphere bred nothing but stress and indigestion—but not hers. Stevie was surrounded by very happy, healthy and harmonious elements.

Her half-hooded gaze surveyed the impressive milieu. Stevie knew that clients, both prospective and established, focused not on such incidentals as floor covering and furniture but on the vividly commanding group of platinum and gold albums that adorned every available wall space.

Those were her badges of honor. In the two years since she had taken total control of her father's business, the number of top sellers certified by the Recording Industry Association of America to her clientele had doubled, as had various other music awards, including the prestigious Grammy and Oscar.

Her hands clutched the chair's upholstered arms; the worn patina on the leather gave evidence of a previous occupant—her father. Her thoughts digressed in nostalgic retrospect. Steven Brandt had groomed his only heir to succeed him in the business of managing recording artists and musicians. It was a labor of love for both parties.

She had grown up amid musicians; her father was a jazz trumpet player and her mother a gospel singer, and this was the world Stevie knew and thrived in. While her own vocal capabilities were poor, she knew how to make music and how to sell it.

Her life had been a mixture of education and business. For all his support, Steven Brandt had been a hard boss, demanding more from his daughter than any other employee and never letting emotions get in the way of business. Stevie added law and accounting courses to bolster her liberal arts degree and signed on for an apprenticeship in broadcast engineering for actual hands-on knowledge of equipment.

When Steven Brandt made his farewell speech at his retirement dinner, the old-timers who controlled

Nashville's Music Row sneered and labeled him a fool to entrust his prosperous thirty-year-old business to his twenty-eight-year-old daughter. A son they could have blessed and helped, but a daughter . . .

Stevie swallowed the sour taste that had suddenly formed in her mouth. Old memories could still taint her triumphs with bitterness. She had realized she might face some discrimination, but Stevie never imagined it would come from those she called friends. Longtime clients and backers had abandoned the agency, as did many seasoned employees.

For a time Stevie felt that she had fallen into an abyss and was aimlessly drifting in a lonely black void. As she struggled to survive her father wisely kept his own counsel, letting the new president run the company without any interference.

Her appetite for a challenge proved to be the armor that shielded and protected her. She persevered and aggressively sought new talent and employees to replace old. Colleagues called her stubborn and bullheaded and she agreed. Like Sinatra, Stephanie Brandt did things her way.

When she was wrong, she took it on the chin and learned, but more often than not she was proved right. Her analytical mind and her uncanny ear for talent slowly began to earn Stevie acceptance along Music Row.

She challenged her father's legacy. Her genius was for choosing creative and innovative singers, groups and musicians who not only turned latex records into gold and platinum but who were adept at multimedia promotions.

Billboard, the nation's leading music trade magazine, had called her the "queen of precious metals"; *Variety* labeled her "Nashville's golden girl." Stevie had concentrated all her energies on one thing—her company. And she was beginning to reap the rewards of her success. She was confident about her choice of key management people and was beginning to delegate some of her authority.

Now, just when Stevie was planning to relax and enjoy life and start focusing attention on herself—"I get Quintin Ward!" she grumbled to herself.

Her eyelid began to twitch uncontrollably. Gossip was a plague that destroyed many a career in the entertainment industry. Stevie's own morals and those of her clients had always been above reproach, but if Quintin Ward's slanderous statements ever made the rounds . . .

A knock interrupted Stevie's speculations. "Here are two aspirins, a cup of hot tea and a cheeseburger." Gloria Lansing placed the filled tray on the wide oak desk. "Plus"—she took a file folder from under her arm—"I found Robert Ward."

Stevie's stockinged heels landed with a thud despite the thickness of the carpet. "You did!"

Her assistant's expression creased into a smile. "Robert Ward works for you," Gloria announced as she settled into the side chair and adjusted her beige skirt.

Viewing her boss's confused, helpless look, she continued. "Bobby, the mailroom go-fer? He comes in Monday, Wednesday and Thursday after school. All legs, dark hair, acne on his chin. Yesterday he had on denim coveralls and a red-striped rugby shirt." Her hands hovered around her ears. "Headphones and a Sony Walkman are part of his anatomy."

A mouthful of burger wedged in Stevie's throat. "And his father has the gall to think I'd seduce a kid who uses Clearasil instead of after-shave!" She reached for the mug of tea. "I barely remember him. How long has this kid been working here?"

Gloria handed her the employment form. "Five months. Don't feel bad," came her soft-spoken directive, "I hired Bobby and didn't make the connection. We've got four mailroom clerks and they all qualify as invisible men."

Between sips of orange spice tea, Stevie perused the neatly printed information sheet. "Address is the same." Her auburn head nodded. "Age: seventeen. Line drawn through the mother's name. Father: Quintin." Her nose wrinkled.

"You can't blame Papa Ward for being upset, Stevie. That florist bill was a hundred bucks."

"Tell me about it! I'm stuck paying it." The file slid down her lap as she remembered various allegations. "He said I gave Bobby presents?" It came out a question; her white teeth worried her lower lip.

"You gave everyone a Christmas bonus," Gloria recounted. A pencil tapped her chin. "Could you have given Bobby any promo albums, T-shirts, maybe a few concert tickets?"

"I don't know." Stevie sank back into her chair, fingers picking at the remains of her dinner, testing the cheeseburger for edibility. "I give those things to everybody. I suppose I could have tossed any one of a dozen so-called *presents* at him."

She rubbed the center of her forehead; the skin felt oily and moist. "Now I'm feeling guilty for every smile, every joke, every breath! I don't remember consciously teasing the kid." Stevie frowned. "You know me: I never lead anyone on."

"I think Bobby's father was just being a father," Gloria soothed. "I'm the mother of a teen-age son, and let me tell you, even when they don't do anything you get wrinkles!" Her lips curved. "Bobby Ward has made you the star of his own personal love fantasy. Puppy love, we used to call it."

Stevie's head tilted to one side, sending a pennant of bronze waves streaming over one shoulder. "Ah, yes, puppy love." She was silent for a moment. "I remember having a crush on an older man," Stevie confessed with a rueful laugh. "Tom Dyer was my high school Latin teacher. What a hunk! I mooned over him for two years, even practiced writing Stephanie Dyer in flowing script in my notebooks." Her complexion took on a rosy glow. "Do you know I still remember what Tom looked like?" came her husky admission. "Tall, blond Viking type with wide shoulders and a narrow waist. I purposely failed tests just to stay after school for some personal attention." Tawny eyebrows lifted in a suggestive manner.

"At night, in bed"—her eyes rolled toward the ceiling—"boy, talk about steamy puberty fantasies!" Stevie grinned at Gloria. "I even saved my allowance and bought him a leather wallet for Christmas. You never saw such an embarrassed man."

"What was your parents' reaction?"

"Pop couldn't understand why I needed two years of Latin; no one spoke it in Nashville. Mom . . . well . . . I think she knew I was having my first love affair, albeit a mental one. Eventually my one-sided dreams died a natural, unresolved death."

Gloria straightened the sleeves on her earth-tone striped blouse. "Now you're in the same position you put your Latin teacher in," she expressed her considered opinion. "The object of someone's affection through no fault of your own."

"You can say that again," Stevie concurred wearily. She straightened in her chair, palms flattened on her desk. "What really galls me, though, is the way Quintin Ward jumped to conclusions. He acted more the adolescent than his son," she announced with feeling. "He attacked me in public. I wasn't even given a chance to say one word in my own defense. He put my head on a chopping block and chopped. He ranted and raved and threatened." Hazel eyes narrowed. "I hate to be threatened. What is moral turpitude anyway?"

Gloria manufactured a shocked expression, hand fluttering against her bosom. "My dear, it's a depraved and shameful act with a minor."

"Quintin Ward's the shameful act," Stevie growled. Her fingers laced the hair back from her temples. "The man needs a course on parenting! It's quite obvious that he's unfamiliar with normal teen-age crushes. These things come and go so quickly. He should learn to communicate with the boy instead of looking for a scapegoat. Me! I get convicted on circumstantial evidence. That's the easy way out!"

Her hands rubbed together in a nervous gesture. "I don't like that. I've got an excellent reputation, and if this gets around . . ." Stevie looked with unseeing eyes at the wall clock. "What time is the gospel concert tonight?"

"Eight-thirty."

"If I leave now, go home and change, I can stop and see Ward and get this matter straightened out before then. Maybe even have a little Dutch-aunt talk with Bobby," Stevie added. "I'll be polite but professional. That should burst Bobby Ward's amorous bubble."

A grin split Gloria's matronly features. "Not afraid to beard the lion in his own den, are you?"

"Lion is right," Stevie retorted sharply, "the man does roar."

"And what does Papa Ward look like?" came the curious inquiry.

Stevie found herself frowning in memory. "Tall.

A few inches on me. Snarly face. Furious dark eyes. Nearly black hair. Roman features. Football build." Her sudden laugh was purely feminine.

"What?" Gloria demanded an explanation.

Hazel eyes gleamed in awareness. "Even after all the yelling and all the swearing, as I watched Quintin Ward stalk out of the restaurant, I remember thinking: There's a man whose rear end could sell a million pairs of Jordache jeans!"

2

~~~~~~~~~~~

The Mercedes's engine purred steadily in neutral while Stephanie Brandt contemplated Quintin Ward's stately southern colonial home. "Charm and dignity." The honeyed words rolled off her tongue. "It's a shame a little didn't rub off on the owner!"

The house's massive columns and pediment gable were dramatic examples of late-eighteenth-century architecture. Antebellum ghosts seemed to dance around the restored plantation, courtesy of the colorful floodlights that cast the giant magnolias, ginkgoes and cedars in shadow.

Through the windshield Stevie pensively regarded the three cars parked ahead of hers on the curved drive. Her hazel eyes stared at the luminous digital clock on the dash; gingered lips puckered in a thoughtful moue. Could Quintin Ward be entertaining dinner guests?

Her hand moved the gearshift from neutral to drive, then suddenly jammed it into park. Stevie snickered in disgust at her concern. Why should she worry about etiquette? The vivid memory of her ruined dinner came into focus. Quintin Ward had no respect for the social graces nor for food. No doubt his guests would welcome an intrusion; the man's idea of gourmet was probably two all-beef patties on a sesame seed bun!

Elegantly manicured fingers pulled the keys from the ignition. Guests or not, Stevie knew it was vital to get this entire situation straightened out immediately. Both her professional and personal reputations were on the line, and it was imperative for the truth to exonerate her.

The Wards, father and son, needed to see everything in proper perspective, and *proper* was the word for this whole affair. *Affair!* She winced and opened the car door. That word had no place in tonight's vocabulary!

The frigid winter air further primed the vibrant woman cocooned in fiery red fox. Stevie felt confident and in control of all her faculties. No matter how Quintin Ward acted, no matter how much the man growled and fumed, she would remain as cool and unflappable as she did when she negotiated recording contracts.

Of course, an impish smile curved her lips; her choice of dress didn't quite match her feelings.

Beneath the perfectly matched pelts was a purely feminine creation of black lace and ruffles. Stevie's smile broadened, her arms squeezing against her sides in a smug gesture. Lace and ruffles would reflect her mood once she was rid of the Wards.

She was going to enjoy the concert at the Opry, attend one of the many parties she had always avoided and have the time of her life. She deserved it!

Her anxious finger pressed against the doorbell. When the chimes played the first four bars of "Tara's Theme" from *Gone With The Wind,* Stevie's calculated hauteur bubbled into laughter.

"Welcome to our open house." Quintin Ward's jubilant greeting and beaming smile slowly disappeared as his dark eyes connected the arresting side tumble of gold-laced auburn curls and attractive, winter-flushed features with a name—Stephanie Brandt. "What the hell are you doing here?"

"Tut, tut, *Master* Ward"—a titian brow lifted in sardonic condemnation—"where's the chivalrous charm that goes with the courtly southern trappings?"

"I'm from Rhode Island," came his clipped rejoinder.

"Then I guess your manners are appropriate for a carpetbagger." Her eyes glittered with an unholy light. Stevie had noted Quintin Ward's initial reaction of masculine appreciation. She found herself indulging in a bold, purely feminine appraisal of her own.

The foyer chandelier created a glowing nimbus

around dark-brown waves that framed strong, Roman features. The brief smile she had witnessed bestowed an appealing warmth that softened the planes and angles of his weathered, sun-bronzed face.

Quintin's broad-shouldered, narrow-waisted, slim-hipped body, which had looked so disturbing in denim work clothes, was just as sexy in the European-style tuxedo. Stevie didn't stop to evaluate the rush of adrenaline that made her act the coquette rather than her normal sedate self.

The toes of her black evening sandals crossed the threshold; her hands lifted to straighten his bow tie. "I came to talk about your son."

Brown eyes blinked into tawny irises that were level with his own. "This . . . this is hardly convenient." For some inexplicable reason Quintin found himself short of breath and stammering.

"It was hardly convenient when you interrupted my dinner." Her palms flattened against the smooth material of his lapels and gave a warning push. Glossed lips formed each word with care. "Now it's *my* turn to talk and *your* turn to listen."

He stared at the feminine hands on his jacket; a muscle worked in his cheek; his voice was tight. "I'm having a party. I have guests."

The heel of her hand dug into his chest. "I'm sure your guests will excuse you." Stevie's manner and tone were unyielding.

"Look. I—"

"Shut up, Mr. Ward. You had your say; now I get mine." Her hand pushed again. "Make your apologies to your guests and then you can make one to me."

"Stevie!" An adolescent male voice squeaked out her name in dual octaves. "I knew you'd come. I just knew you'd accept my invitation." Bobby Ward's lanky evening-suited frame sidled next to his father. "Dad, this is my boss, Stevie Brandt." An oversize grin stretched his lips. "Oh, wow. I can't believe it." His childish face grew mottled with his excitement. "This is wonderful!"

Her smile was feeble. For the life of her she couldn't remember being invited to the Wards' open house. And even if she had, she certainly would never have made an appearance.

"Rob, you never told me Miss Brandt was to be our guest tonight." Quintin's congenial voice belied the rough hands that aided Stevie out of her fur coat. "I don't recall getting your RSVP." The question was expelled through even white teeth.

Bobby shrugged the answer. "I'm surprised Stevie even found the card I left under her calendar. Her desk looks like the aftereffects from an A-bomb! It's always piled with demos, LPs, discs, tapes, folders, posters . . ." His brown gaze shifted to his red-haired employer. The soft architecture of midnight faille flowed and defined her womanly contours; the dress's plunging neckline was saved from total impropriety by layers of black lace. "Oh, wow, you look gorgeous!"

A weak smile etched Stevie's lips. She watched Bobby turn five shades of red, his expression much like the basset hound her uncle owned. *The kid really has it bad. Now, why couldn't I inspire this type of response from a male who uses a razor more than once a week!*

Mascaraed lashes shielded her glance at Quintin. The intensity of his feelings was all too visible on his face. *If looks could kill.* Stevie shook off a chill that had little to do with the winter temperature.

The melodic door chimes heralded more arrivals. "Aren't those wild?" Bobby grinned. "A friend of Dad's had those made to celebrate the renovation of Cedar Hill."

"Cedar Hill?"

"We're not quite Belle Meade," he said, laughing. His hand made a wide sweeping gesture. "Let me give you the grand tour." Turning his back on his father, Bobby hesitated for a moment before letting shaky fingers slide along Stevie's bare arm to grip her elbow.

Stevie gave a backward glance in Quintin's direction, took note of his scowling expression and decided she was damned either way. "Belle Meade once presided over five thousand acres. How does Cedar Hill compare?" came her pleasant inquiry as Bobby led her across the mammoth entrance foyer with its black and white marble floor and open twisted staircase.

"Back in 1850 this manor house was queen to about a thousand meadowland acres. Five years ago Dad saved the place from a wrecking ball," Bobby told her. "Vandals and vagrants had set small fires; windows were glassless holes; the roof had more birds' nests than shingles. Dad liked the ten acres of land; we both hated living in an apartment, so . . ."

"The rest, as they say, is history," Stevie supplied, viewing with approval the ornate powder room, with its double marble sink and French toile wallpaper. "Who did all the decorating?"

"Dad and I. We've been poring over the books at the historical society, hunting through antique stores looking for odds and ends, period pieces, good reproductions." Bobby pushed open the study door. "There's quite a bit of history in some of our furniture."

There was no doubt in Stevie's mind that the den was Quintin Ward's private domain: The room looked like him. Massive, bold, solid. From the leather-topped desk to the oversize hide furnishings to the beautiful collection of books, their tooled bindings displayed to best advantage in the floor-to-ceiling bookcases.

Carved doors led from the study to the formal parlor with its arched windows defined by Doric columns. Walls were a mellow gold accented with cream-painted woodwork; chandelier wall sconces highlighted the polished wood floor, Oriental carpet, and a comfortable mix of Georgian tables and chairs combined with contemporary sofas and lamps.

"You've really done a remarkable job." Stevie meant the compliment. She followed Bobby into the large gathering room that was obviously the center of family activity. From the ornate fireplace blue-gold–tipped flames crackled and hissed a greeting, inviting the growing number of guests to warm themselves. "Do you play?" Stevie's auburn head nodded toward the baby grand piano in the opposite corner.

"Dad and I are taking lessons," Bobby grumbled the reply. "I like to listen to music—not do those endless scales."

Stevie favored him with a maternal smile. "I think you'll appreciate music more when you learn how it's made. The most joyous sounds come from the emotions"—her hand patted his breast pocket—"and from the heart."

"Do . . . do you play?" His eyes were riveted on the feminine hand that touched him.

"Yes. Piano, drums and guitar." A low chuckle escaped her. "My first crib was a blanket-lined bass case," Stevie informed Bobby. "My mother was a gospel singer and my father a jazz trumpet player. We were quite the gypsies, going from one gig to another. I've always been surrounded by music; I don't know anything else."

"Your life is so . . . so . . ." he groped for the right word—"awesome."

Again Stevie found herself in the uncomfortable position of being worshiped by puppy-dog eyes. Clearing her throat, she made her tone clipped and professional. "Bobby, you're failing in your duties as a tour guide." Her elbow prompted him into motion.

The dining room shimmered under large, ornate mirrors and a breathtaking chandelier that seemed an infinite cascade of crystal icicles. The banquet-size table was graced by a decorative ice sculpture and a bountiful array of foods.

"The kitchen is totally twentieth century, right down to the microwave." Bobby's fingers ruffled through his dark, shaggily wavy hair. "I'd show it to you, but the caterers have thrown me out twice." The toe of his black dress shoe made a path in the low nap of the Oriental carpet. He took a deep breath and grabbed her wrist. "Let's go up the back staircase."

She coughed. "Huh . . . well . . ." Stevie found that her matter-of-fact attitude had deserted her. "Shouldn't you . . . shouldn't we go back to the living room? Your doorbell has played the entire overture, and I imagine your father could use your help with the guests." A hopeful smile accompanied her request as she successfully disengaged her wrist.

"Dad's fine. He loves to play host." Ignoring her stuttered protests, Bobby took Stevie's hand and began climbing the polished wooden steps. "The second-floor lounge opens for a spectacular view of the main gathering area. We had a twenty-foot Christmas tree this year."

Bobby was right, Stevie acknowledged a few moments later. The view was breathtaking. Even with the lack of artificial yuletide glitter, the main floor's family room was a colorful palette, resplendent, courtesy of chandeliers, fireplace and elegant furnishings.

While leaning over the wooden balcony railing, Stevie discovered quite a few familiar faces among the crowd. She was acquainted with the local politicians, very friendly with the entertainers and had had social conversations with some of the other guests.

How strange that Quintin Ward and I haven't met before, Stevie thought. Her hazel eyes bridged the distance, focusing on the man in question. To her surprise she found herself under the same scrutiny, but the harsh lines etched on Quintin's face denoted a less than favorable reaction.

"My dad's bedroom is the entire left wing," Bobby's voice interrupted her musings. "Mine is over here."

She looked at the hand that again covered hers. "I'm too *old* to fall for that etchings line," came her wry scold. She realized she had failed to make her point when Bobby blinked dumbly and uttered, "Huh?"

He flipped on the wall switch; the ceiling light flooded the room. "Look how I framed all the posters you gave me and . . . and . . ." Bobby riffled through the papers on his bookcase-topped desk—"here's that review you asked me to do."

"Review?" Three vertical lines ridged her smooth forehead. "I . . . I asked you to do a review?"

"On Monday, when I picked up those Express

Mail packages," Bobby prompted. "You handed me the Pit Stops' newest LP and asked for my opinion."

"Well. I, uh . . ." Stevie staggered in confusion and felt in need of a chair. Since the only one in the room was covered with clothes and books, she stumbled toward the edge of the bed. "Bobby"— her tone was kind—"when I said, 'Let me know what you think of this,' I never meant for you to give me a written report."

"Oh, don't worry. I didn't take any time away from my studies. I knew you'd be concerned about that." He balanced his right knee on the bedspread, his hands curved around Stevie's shoulders. "I know how you feel about me."

Stevie stared at him, her eyes wide and wondering. "How I feel about you?" She was becoming uncomfortably aware of the fact that she was no longer in control of this situation. Bobby Ward had every intention of bringing his fantasy to life.

"I've read all the books. I'm not stupid. I can read the signs. I understand body language. I know the signals a woman sends."

"You do?" Her tongue washed dry lips. "What signals have I been sending you?"

His expression was once again dreamy. "The way your face lights up with that special smile every time I come into your office."

I smile at everybody, came her silent disclaimer. *I spent three years wearing braces just so I could smile at everybody.*

"You're just so eager to see me. I'm trying to arrange my after-school schedule so I can be with you every day."

Oh, Bobby, of course I'm eager to see you. . . . You bring me the mail!

"All the gifts you've given me." His hand fluttered around the room. "The posters, the records, the tapes, the concert tickets."

They're purely promotional. . . . All the staff gets them.

"Last week you told me to call you Stevie." Bobby's hands curved around her shoulders. "And then there was that kiss you gave me at the Christmas party." A long sigh escaped him.

"Bobby." Stevie finally became vocal. Conscious of his fragile ego, she tempered her words with a smile. "Everyone calls me Stevie. I'm in a business that invites fast familiarity, and it's easier than *Miss* or *Ms.,* and I hate *ma'am.*" She patted his arm. "And about that Christmas kiss. Wasn't it under the mistletoe in the employees' lounge?" came her gentle reminder. "I must have kissed all the male employees!"

"That's what I love about you"—he sighed again—"you're so . . . easy to talk to, so relaxed."

"For sure," Stevie muttered. She took a deep breath and became more diligent. "Bobby, I'm afraid you have . . . ohhh!" Her hands pushed against him, trying to fend off his advancing arms. "Bobby! Bobby!" Stevie managed to turn her head just in time to let his lips bounce off her jaw instead of her mouth.

"Robert," Quintin Ward's deep voice intoned from the open doorway, "your godparents are downstairs; they'd like to see you. Now."

With a hastily whispered "We'll get together later," Bobby scrambled off the bed and out of the bedroom.

Quintin's contemptuous appraisal made Stevie feel unclean. For a brief moment her composure wavered, but then she regained her poise. "Mr. Ward, I know how this must look, but—"

"Shut up, Miss Brandt." His voice was an animal's snarl. His rugged physique towered like a monolith over Stevie's seated form. "I've witnessed the truth," he raged, the veins in his neck bulging over the collar of his white dress shirt. "You lured that boy up here. God knows what would have happened if I hadn't come upstairs. And in my own house!"

"Mr. . . . Mr. Ward!" Stevie struggled to stand but found herself roughly pushed back onto the candlewick bedspread.

"I don't want to hear your lies." His face was nearly purple, his hands clenching and unclenching just inches from her slender throat. "I want you to get the hell out of here. Now." Quintin turned and stalked out the door.

Still on her back, Stevie regained control over her erratic breathing. She stared at the bedroom ceiling, her eyes attempting to make order from the intricate maze of patterns on the acoustical tiles. It seemed an easier task than the one she was now faced with.

"What we have here is the proverbial molehill built into a mountain. Actually the Himalayas." Her voice was surprisingly calm. "Bobby needs to be told that he's created something out of nothing." Stevie decided to make that correction Monday afternoon in her office.

Seated behind her massive desk, clad in gray flannel and using her brusque, no-nonsense voice, she could be quite intimidating. If Bobby failed to understand that what he perceived as sexual interest was merely her friendly, informal attitude toward her employees, then Stevie would simply fire him! Sometimes you had to be cruel to be kind.

Speaking of cruel . . . The word reminded Stevie of Quintin Ward's ruthless behavior. She rolled off the bed and straightened her dress. Her fingertips rubbed his rough touch from her bare arm. *Now, there's a man who needs a good swift kick right in his assertions!*

Stevie smiled at her image in the dresser mirror; she leaned closer, letting her fingers comb and fluff the fiery curls. *I realize you're concerned about your child—and I sympathize with you, Quintin Ward—but your attitude and actions need some major adjustments. And like any good Tennessee woman, I'm going to volunteer to make them!*

She used the extension telephone to make a quick call to arrange to have one of her associates attend the gospel concert at the "Grand Ole Opry." Then, with the spirit and daring of her Tennessee ancestors, Stevie proceeded down the back stairs to wage war on a Yankee.

Her first stop was the dining room. She decided to avail herself of Quintin's hospitality. Her smile broadened as she filled the white china plate with assorted tempting canapés and hors d'oeuvres. . . . Nothing like biting the hand that feeds you.

When the white-jacketed bartender inquired as to her pleasure, Stevie was thoughtful for a moment, then decided to go for broke: "Sour mash" —one hazel eye winked—"neat." Glass and plate firmly in hand, she returned to the house's main living area and allowed herself to relax and participate.

Squatting before the hearth, Quintin expertly used the brass poker to check the security of two new logs before he repositioned the metal safety screen. He brushed off his hands and turned to survey the laughing, chattering guests that milled around him. Everyone had food and/or drinks; the stereo was loud enough to be heard but soft enough to allow for conversations; and from the high spirits that abounded, the evening looked like a success.

Parties were not his forte. Building the houses that held the parties—that was where his talents lay. Tonight, however, was his premiere as both builder and host. The restoration and renovation of Cedar Hill had taken more than just his skill as a carpenter. He had used his engineering and architectural knowledge to duplicate the beauty and recreate the ambience that once flourished in this antebellum mansion.

Quintin felt Cedar Hill was more than a house. It

was home. A home that stood as a symbol of togetherness and a newly discovered awareness of his son. His dark gaze found Robert, who was slowly nursing the one drink he had been allotted that evening.

A proud paternal smile lightened Quintin's features. Rob looked good. The tuxedo seemed to add an elegant virility to the seventeen-year-old's slim, angular frame. Quintin massaged his jaw; at least those headphones Rob always wore were put away for one night and his feet sported real shoes instead of sneakers.

His son not only looked good, he was good. Excellent school grades, health foods, no signs of drugs. What more could a parent ask? Quintin rescued his Scotch from the ornately carved mantle and pondered that question. He'd like Rob to be more like himself; he'd like Rob to work at his side. Quintin had always dreamed of a sign that would read Ward and Son Construction Company.

Rob's interest, however, was music. Not the making of it but the business of music. Big business that was the heart of Nashville. A business that was filled with addicts and alcoholics and vampires who greedily sucked young blood and devoured souls.

Quintin blanketed his son under a protective gaze—a gaze that was shattered by the sudden appearance of Stephanie Brandt. Hypnotized, he watched her mingle with his other guests. *The arrogance of that woman!* An underlying rawness blistered each word.

He stalked her every movement. But the longer

Quintin watched Stevie, the more fascinated he became. His eyes centered on the tender curve of her left ear glimpsed through teasing auburn tendrils, and the delicate ripple of muscle that flowed along her slender arm when she lifted her glass.

His gaze found pleasure in viewing the tall, well-curved feminine form beneath her designer gown. The ruffled layers of black lace that formed the provocative décolletage only succeeded in heightening the impact of her full creamy breasts. Quintin's hand tightened around his glass as he remembered how enticing Stephanie Brandt had looked on the bed upstairs.

The Scotch was quickly tossed down a parched masculine throat. He hoped the liquor would dull and depress this surprising libidinous reaction. Quintin looked into his empty old-fashioned glass and then to the earthy female intruder. The tremors were still reverberating. Stephanie Brandt *had* to go! He slammed the glass on the mantle and strode purposefully across the room.

"Allow me to escort you to your coat."

Despite the harsh voice that growled in her ear and the pressure from a hand on the small of her back, Stevie's smile never wavered. Gold-shadowed eyelids lowered to let black lashes flutter against an ivory complexion. "If it isn't our charming host." She turned her head, the cascade of titian curls catching him full in the face. "The Mayor and I were just discussing your talents."

Quintin looked over her shoulder and somehow found the courage to smile a greeting at the politician. "Good evening, sir, glad you could make it. Would you excuse Miss Brandt for a moment?" His palm cupped her elbow and steered her forward.

"Please, Quintin, you're making me drop my shrimp puffs!"

His broad, elegantly clad torso moved to block her path. "You were supposed to leave."

She feigned confusion. "Why would I want to do that? I'm having a wonderful time. Good food"—she lifted her plate—"good liquor"—she toasted him with her drink—"and such a congenial host." The glass balanced on her plate, Stevie raised her thumb and forefinger and pinched Quintin's cheek. Hazel eyes flirted. "Now I see where Bobby inherited his charm." It was a cheap shot, she silently admitted, but the man had it coming.

Watching Quintin's face grow ashen, Stevie suddenly felt contrite. Hell! If she were the parent with the overactive teen-ager, she'd probably act the insane fool herself. She took a deep breath, her expression serious. "Look, Mr. Ward, why don't we adjourn to your study and talk. I really think—"

"Stevie! Stevie Brandt, is that you?" Her good intentions were interrupted by a music publisher. "Congratulations." Darren Newman grabbed her hand and pumped her arm. "I see you've got a nominee in every category of the American Music Awards." His elbow nudged Quintin's. "This lady is dyn-o-mite." He cocked his forefinger at Stevie. "Are you going to LA for the awards?"

"I usually do. My clients will be there," she promised.

"Has Quintin showed you his new digital audio playback system?" Darren inquired as he looked toward his host. "Stevie was one of the first to have her clients record on the laser disks."

"I only have the classics," Quintin returned coolly. "Is Pavarotti or Bernstein one of your clients?"

"No, but Brandt Associates just handled the laser recording of Handel's *Messiah* by the London Symphony Orchestra," came her equally icy rebuttal. "I'm always amazed at the superior technical quality of the disks; the dynamic range is unsurpassed, and of course they are impervious to wear."

"Well, it was a brilliant move." Darren grinned at her. "While the recording companies were handing out their standard repertoire, you jumped to Europe and beat them. I'm going to be calling you to set up an appointment; I think we can talk some business." When her red head nodded in approval, Darren slapped Quintin on the back, muttered "Nice party" and disappeared into the crowd.

Before Stevie could resume her conversation with Quintin Ward, two more acquaintances discovered her presence. She smiled shyly when they commented on how beautiful she looked, answered their inquiries about the health of her parents by mentioning that the elder Brandts were enjoying the tropic delights of Hawaii and accepted their good wishes for her continued business success.

During this exchange, Bobby Ward had gravitated to her side. Not wanting to further agitate Quintin, Stevie sent his son to the bar on the pretext of refreshing her drink. "Let's go to your study for that little talk before Bobby comes back," she directed, and before he could form a response, Stevie wound her arm around his and steered a path through the crowd.

Stevie launched her verbal attack before the door latch clicked in the lock. "Let me make one thing perfectly clear, Mr. Ward. I do not now have, nor have I ever had, sexual"—millions of shivers bubbled over her skin—"designs on your son. In fact, until late today, I wasn't even aware that Robert Ward existed. He is just another invisible mail clerk in my building."

Her bold affront continued. "I think the kid is just starved for female affection." She paced back and forth in front of Quintin's militarylike stance. "Although why he didn't pick a high school cheerleader, I don't know. Maybe he's shy with girls his own age.

"My office staff is like an extension of my family." The black skirt rustled around her ankles. "We laugh, we joke, the atmosphere is very informal." Stevie stopped pacing to view his stoic features. "Bobby has misinterpreted my every smile, my every statement. He thinks all those freebee promotionals were personal gifts."

Her raised palm stopped his forthcoming interruption. "Mr. Ward, you have my word. Monday I will sit Bobby down, explain the facts of life to him, and if push comes to shove, I'll just have to terminate his employment." Stevie favored him with an encouraging smile. "Will that make you happy?"

"So you weren't even aware of Rob?" Quintin arched a disbelieving brow. "Then why turn up on our doorstep all dressed for a party, or is this"—his finger flicked a black-lace ruffle—"your usual evening attire?"

Stevie emitted a low growl. "I was on my way to a concert at the 'Opry.' I made the time to come to straighten out this misunderstanding."

"Really?" His dark head nodded cockily. "And did I misunderstand that little tryst upstairs?"

"Tryst!" Her hands curled into impotent fists that punched the air. "Haven't you heard a word I said? Damn it, but you are a stubborn, bullheaded, totally—"

"I saw you kissing my son."

"Kissing!" Her head reeled back in shock.

"I know what I saw, Miss Brandt."

"I was not kissing your son," Stevie hissed. She stood on her toes; her face was nose-to-nose with Quintin's. "Your son gave me a peck on the cheek." Noting his disbelieving look, her hazel eyes turned dangerous. "This, Mr. Ward, is what I call a kiss!"

Her fingers grasped the lapels on his evening jacket, crushing the expensive fabric into her palms. She leaned against him; the force of her body bent him backward over his desk. Her mouth slanted over his half-parted lips, effectively smothering his astonishment. Her tongue made a quick intimate taunt, finding enjoyment in the subtle taste of Scotch.

When she realized what she was doing, Stevie pushed herself free. "Now you know the difference." Her eyes radiated an intoxicated glow. "I don't need to seduce boys, Quintin Ward." With a swish of black lace she turned and disappeared out of the door.

Quintin stared at the white-knuckled hands that still gripped the edges of the desk. He was at a loss to understand what had happened. He had been in control; he had been so positive, and then . . . His forefinger smoothed his lips. He had never encountered a woman like Stephanie Brandt before, but he'd certainly like to again.

"Hey, Dad?" Robert Ward's dark head poked into the study. "What happened? Stevie grabbed her coat from the closet and ran out the front door."

"Rob, come in here a moment." Quintin put an arm around his son. "Listen to me, I want—"

"Wait a minute, Dad." He pulled away. "Did you say something to Stevie?" Rob demanded. His dark eyes sparked in a silent warning. "You know how I feel about her."

Quintin chose his words with care. "Look, son, these feelings you have for Miss Brandt are . . . well"—he took a deep breath—"she just doesn't think of you in that way."

"You . . . you *did* say something to her!" Bobby slammed his right fist into his left palm. "You have no right to interfere in our relationship."

"There is no relationship." His tone was soft but with an underlying edge of authority.

"Yes there is, Dad." Bobby took a deep breath. "And it's going to continue. You're not being fair. . . ."

Quintin stood up and towered to his full six-foot height. "I don't have to be fair; I'm your father. You're my son and you're underage. I know my rights."

"Rights?" Rob's voice splintered. "You may pay for my education, my clothes, my food, but damn it, you don't own me. You can't control my mind or my heart!"

"Don't talk to me in that tone, Robert, I'm your father."

"I have rights too," his son barked defensively. "If . . . if you don't leave me and Stevie alone . . . I'll . . . I'll leave." Yanking open the study door, Rob threw a backward glance of pure malice at his father. "That's a promise, Father. If you don't back off, you'll find yourself alone."

3

~~~~~~~~~~

The pounding started at three A.M. It took Stevie a full minute to realize that her town house was not being shaken by an earthquake. Someone or something was bludgeoning her front door!

"All right! All right!" Scrambling out of bed, Stevie tripped over an errant shoe and continued to stumble her way across the darkened living room. "I'm coming! I'm coming!" Her fingers froze against the cold metal dead bolt as common sense invaded her sleep-drugged brain.

She took note of the quiet. There were no fire, police or ambulance sirens or any other sounds that could be equated with a life-threatening disturbance. One of her neighbors could be in trouble, Stevie reflected, but then again this could be a ruse.

As one hazel eye focused on the security peephole, her hand flipped on the outside porch light. The amber light illuminated her nemesis of eight hours before. "Quintin Ward!" Her own fist hit the carved wood panel. Stevie opened the front door, yelled an uncivil "Go home!" and then slammed it shut.

Again the door reverberated under a barrage of fists. "Please, Miss Brandt, it's life and death."

Stevie counted to ten before twisting the knob. "Yours, I hope." Her mood switched from sarcastic to self-righteous. "Look, Mr. Ward, I've really had it. Enough is enough. Stop harassing me or I'll call my lawyer and—" Her threat bubbled into wispy white puffs that feebly attempted to warm the frigid night air.

Quintin Ward looked like a beaten man. His tall, broad-shouldered physique appeared crippled under an invisible weight. The expertly tailored evening suit had lost its glamour. The black bow tie hung loosely around the open neck of the white shirt, while the jacket and slacks were creased and rumpled.

Most profound was the change in his facial appearance. Stevie noted the cast of his complexion—gray-green despite the amber outdoor lamp—the dark smudges under his eyes and the once proud Roman features that now looked defeated by pain and fear.

A sympathetic sigh escaped her as she ushered him into the foyer. "What's the problem?" Realizing that she lacked a bathrobe, Stevie folded her arms across the front of her thin ivory silk sleep shirt.

"It's Rob. He's . . ." The words were dragged from deep within Quintin. ". . . he's threatened to run away."

"Oh, God. Come on in." She half-pushed, half-pulled him into the living room, stopping only to turn up the thermostat and snap on the table lamp. "Tell me what happened."

Quintin collapsed onto the black velvet modular sofa. "Rob saw you rush out of the house tonight." His tongue swept his dry lips. "He came into the study and accused me of trying to break up your relationship."

Her low whine interrupted. "We don't have a relationship to break up!" Flopping next to him, Stevie closed her eyes and massaged her forehead, hoping to halt the tension that was regrouping to stage another headache.

"Rob wouldn't listen to anything," Quintin continued, not even acknowledging her interruption. "He said I didn't own him. I couldn't run his life, tell him what to do, what to think or whom to see. And if I tried, he'd run away." Trembling hands made a weary pass over his face. "Damn, but I've made such a mess of everything."

"Calm down. Calm down." Her fingers gripped his upper arm. She struggled to find the words that would comfort him. "Now look, Mr. Ward, people say and do all sorts of stupid things they don't mean when they're angry." Stevie swallowed hard;

remembering her own slip into insanity in his study. "Bobby was probably just blowing off a little steam, trying to show you he's not a kid, being—"

"I know he's not a kid!" Quintin rounded. "That's ninety percent of the problem. He's too damn big to spank, and what's the use of sending him to his room?" he demanded with a sneer. "Do you know how impossible it is to discipline and control a teen-ager?"

"I'm sure it is," her husky contralto strove to soothe, "but maybe you're approaching this the wrong way. I don't think control is quite what a parent should do."

"Well, thank you, Dr. Spock," came his sarcastic rejoinder.

Stevie's mauve-tinted fingernails curved into the material of his sleeve. She could feel the tempered strength of his biceps. "Wait just one damn minute, Mr. Ward." Her tone was dangerous, her eyes slicked by ice. "You came knocking on my door. I didn't ask to be put in the middle."

Quintin disengaged her hand; his dark gaze flamed under another inner eruption of anger. "Lady, you're the one who created this entire fiasco!"

"Me? You're crazy! I—" Her sputtered objection was vehemently conquered by further rude accusations.

Stevie became aware that Quintin Ward had gone from beaten to belligerent. She realized that anything said in her defense would have little, if any, effect on the man. So she gave up.

Curling herself comfortably into the plush cushions, she decided to play psychiatrist. Let the man bellow and rant, came her silent decision; she'd just sit and listen without interrupting his raging soliloquy.

"Rob and I had a wonderful relationship until he started working for you." Quintin's long legs circumnavigated the massive glass coffee table in three paces. "He was content and happy in the normal world until you showed him what he was missing. You're everything I'm not. You're everything I told Rob he couldn't have."

A derisive index finger jabbed toward Stevie. "Let's face it, you're glamorous and exciting and so is your world. I'm a construction engineer who works with his hands, and there's nothing glitzy about two-by-fours, shingles and copper plumbing.

"You jet around the world and live among the . . ." His fingers made quote marks in the air. ". . . beautiful people and know all the stars. I'm a homebody who meets an occasional celebrity or politician when I build an addition on their house.

"You . . . you're . . ." He tugged at the hem of her nightshirt. ". . . silk and designer clothes. I'm denim and flannel and damn uncomfortable in a tuxedo. For all its antebellum charm, our house is nothing compared to this sleek, contemporary villa." He gestured at the indoor columns, the elegant decorator accessories and the modern furnishings.

"And my party tonight"—a rueful laugh escaped

him; the toe of his shoe scuffed along the top of the black and ivory Ming patterned Chinese rug— "how can that compare to the notorious, infamous orgies the music world is noted for? I've read about your raunchy get-togethers: everyone blowing their brains out with cocaine, nude hot-tub encounters, naked women in cages, naked men swinging from chandeliers."

Completely drained, Quintin stumbled back to the sofa. He was so engrossed in his own self-pity that he failed to notice the change in Stevie. Her previously unperturbed expression was forbidding. "Bobby's a normal, healthy, adventurous kid. You represent the ultimate candy shop and he wants to gorge.

"Stephanie Brandt, *you* are the Lorelei." His thumb lifted her chin. "You're the forbidden fruit. Sophisticated, alluring, provocative. You fill him with wonder. You're a thrilling mystery that he wants to solve." His tone was suddenly bitter. "The sins of the father.

"I know the lure of an older woman." Of their own volition, Quintin's hands slid into Stevie's sleep-disheveled copper hair. His calloused fingers found themselves hugged in the luxury of her silken curls. "I know what my son is wishing when he stares into your eyes; I know the way he hungers for your lips; I know what he dreams and fantasizes when he looks at your body."

Quintin stared at her for what seemed to him to be forever. Chestnut eyes began to rapidly blink away old memories. "God, I could use some coffee." He rubbed his jaw, the dark stubble of his beard scratching against his palm.

"Coffee? Coffee!" In one fluid movement Stevie exploded to her feet. "Do you think our sharing a nice hot cup of roasted Colombian mountain beans is going to make everything you said all right?"

When he opened his mouth, she raised a hand in warning. "Don't you dare utter one sound, Quintin Ward. You've really got some nerve! You think you know so damn much about everything. So damn much about me and my world."

Her upraised palm drew back as if it intended to slap him. "So far you've been doing all the talking and jumping to all the conclusions. Now it's my turn to talk—and you, by God, are going to listen."

Pushing up the long sleeves on her nightshirt, Stevie paced in front of him and tried to organize an effective rebuttal. "First, my glamorous, exciting life full of jets and"—her fingers made quotation marks in the air—"beautiful people. At times, yes, it is glamorous and exciting." Her auburn head nodded in agreement. "But that's the nature of the entertainment business. To get to that end, however, takes a hell of a lot of hard work.

"I don't have a nine-to-five job, Mr. Ward. As a matter of fact, in the past few years I've had little time to call my own. Brandt Associates has forty-three employees with branch offices in LA, New York and London. I have to know who, where and what's going on all the time. I make the final decisions. Not only do I worry about my employees, but I control the careers and the lives of the people I manage."

She leveled an accusing gaze at him. "Contrary to what that pea-size brain of yours may be thinking, Mr. Ward, I did not sleep my way to the top. My father groomed me from the day I was born to take over his company, and I did so willingly.

"As a woman in a predominantly male-oriented business, I've had a long, hard struggle to be taken seriously. I can't act like a groupie. I have to be tough and hard-nosed. I operate by a certain set of rules, and when someone in my organization—be it employee or client—fails to conform to my standards, I fire them."

Stevie raked back her hair. "I respect myself and my reputation. That's one of the reasons I went to your house last night, Mr. Ward. Your erroneous and slanderous accusations could damage the Brandt name, and that means too much to me."

Clearing her throat, she continued. "As far as my house and my clothes are concerned"—Stevie drew herself up to her full height—"this place is decorated to suit me and my current life-style. When I change, it changes."

Her fingers traced the bronze braiding on the lapels of her lingerie. "I wear silk no more easily than I wear denim and cotton or my fleece jogging suit. I'm a woman who sweats, Mr. Ward, not perspires!"

Hazel eyes glowed like polished agates; full breasts heaved beneath the fluid opulence of their ivory silk covering. "You've convinced yourself that

I'm evil incarnate. Those wild, infamous parties? They're not mine. I run a very straight and rather boring operation. When I serve 'coke,' it's in a glass, not a plastic bag, and the only orgy I've ever had was with a pepperoni pizza.

"Maybe some of the musicians and groups I manage don't look like the people in your high school yearbook, but that doesn't make them less than dirt." Her intonation was decidedly icy. "They are bright and decent and hardworking, and they function on talent rather than illegal substances.

"Finally, as to your son"—the muscles in her face grew hard; her voice was almost totally devoid of any emotion—"I have never wished for, never dreamed of, never alluded to, never had and never will have any kind of relationship, sexual or otherwise, with Robert. I was not attracted to seventeen-year-old boys when I was seventeen, and I'm not attracted to them now. On Monday your son will no longer work for Brandt Associates and you will no longer intrude in my life.

"You want coffee, Mr. Ward?" Stevie walked over to the burgundy lacquer wall unit, pulled down the desk panel and then stalked back.

Her fingers yanked Quintin's hand at the wrist. "Go buy yourself a cup." She slapped a dollar bill into his palm. "You have one minute to get out of my sight." She turned her back on his dumbstruck expression; her bare foot tapped the carpet with ever increasing impatience.

Stevie's feminine radar was tuned into Quintin Ward's every movement. Her ears acknowledged his ragged dispelling of breath. She listened as hesitant footsteps shuffled along the carpet to the tiled foyer. After a moment the front door opened and all other sounds ceased until the final click of the lock.

Only then was the tension Stevie had built up released, leaving her shaking and spent. Lying on her stomach, eyes closed, face resting against the velvet upholstery, Stevie forced herself to relax and tried to make her body return to its normal equilibrium. Instead her mind drifted and darted in light-headed confusion. The main preoccupation? Quintin Ward.

Clenched fists pummeled the cushions as she indulged in a childish temper tantrum. Still teeming with a wealth of unspoken defenses, Stevie almost wished she hadn't kicked the man out. How dare he condemn her life-style, her clothes, her home, her very existence!

"Damn you, Quintin Ward, you know nothing about the real Stephanie Brandt!" The outspoken declaration caught Stevie by surprise. Incredulity crowded out all the other emotions as she tried to make sense of her own frustration.

If anyone else had attacked her with those allegations, Stevie ruefully admitted, her reactions would have been quite different. She would have cloaked herself in her usual impervious armor, assumed an aloof, regal attitude and politely asked them to vacate the premises.

But Quintin Ward had elicited an emotional response. Stevie had been driven by an overwhelming urge to correct his misinformation, to prove that she was above reproach, to make him believe she was his moral equal. While she had often had to prove her business prowess, this was the first time she had ever felt the need to defend her character. Was it just a matter of pride?

Stevie found it easy to invoke Quintin Ward's mental image, even easier to remember his touch. For all Quintin's roughness his hands had been gentle, lifting and fluffing her hair like a soft, tropical breeze. The calloused thumb that had sculpted her chin and jawline was tender and decidedly stimulating.

As her body stretched and conformed to the curve of the sofa, she imagined the luxuriant upholstery that caressed her flushed, tingling skin was Quintin's virile flesh. Her heightened senses reeled under the vivid memory of his spicy cologne.

Her fingers bit into the cushions, feeling not the foam but a man's sinewy strength. She wanted to feel again the sensuous pressure of his lips against hers. She yearned for a kiss that would be shared.

Yearned? Stevie shivered under the resurgence of this long-dormant emotion. *You, the Iron Maiden,* an inner voice taunted with delight. *How lovely to know that you can still feel and even want again. What a marvelous feminine reaction!*

Her eyes narrowed into distrustful slits. "A lot of good that marvelous feminine reaction has done you so far," Stevie hissed in defiance.

But you are older and infinitely wiser, claimed

her conscience, *and this man could care less about your business.*

"This man could care less about me!" she sassed quickly. "Why him?" Her words were barely audible, but Stevie's feelings were quite distinct. Rolling on her back, she stared at the ceiling and jeered at fate. "Quintin Ward hates me."

What rankled more than any of his accusations was the impression that even when Quintin was touching her, he had been thinking of someone else. "You're jealous!" Stevie chided herself. "You wanted to be the center of his attention!"

Shaky hands threaded through her hair. Damn it! What was the matter with her anyway? These were not her normal feelings. Maybe her glands were out of whack.

A wry smile twisted her lips. "Probably from disuse," she muttered. "Some 'new woman' you are!" While she was liberated in many other areas, Stevie acknowledged that she was very old-fashioned in her ideas of morality.

Sex to her was not casual or impersonal. She had never been one to frequent singles bars; she just never understood the language and she had enough self-esteem not to want to wake up next to a stranger.

Quintin Ward had been right about one thing: she did travel in a fast world. Drugs and alcohol abounded, as did recreational sex, contract marriages, live-in lovers, "palimony" suits and divorces. Maybe it was living and working in this climate that had made her guard against superficial alliances.

Stevie wanted something lasting. She wanted to emulate her parents, who were celebrating thirty-five years of marital togetherness. "Face it, lady," came her rueful announcement, "you're an out-of-date seventy-eight LP in a world littered with modern forty-fives!"

Her business position had been the major influence on her love life. She invested so much of herself in her job that there was very little left to share with a man. Stevie inherited all the professional stress previously reserved for men. It was difficult to keep her feminine side visible because of her business position. Her career required a goal-oriented, structured state of mind that demanded independence, not intimacy.

For the last five years, and even more diligently in the last two, Stevie had banished love and romance from her life. Oh, there had been the usual promotional dates and party appearances, but they occurred with friends and associates, not lovers. After a day filled with appointments, professional pressures and conflicts, the only thing Stevie languished for was a long soak in her Jacuzzi so she could decompress.

That was her life and she had been happy. Until yesterday, until last night, until Quintin Ward. *Why him?* She repeated that question, hazel eyes looking for answers in the artistic details on the plaster ceiling moulding.

She certainly knew handsomer men. Her lips

curved upward. Quintin's face could easily be carved from granite. And that Jekyll-and-Hyde temper of his! The man was bold and belligerent, stubborn and willful and unfeeling.

Stevie quickly corrected herself. No, Quintin Ward was not unfeeling. As a matter of fact it was the depth of his emotions that she found so attractive—so compelling.

The furnace kicked on; warm air drifted like a blanket to cover her supine form. *Attractive and compelling.* A series of yawns escaped Stevie. Her eyelids refused to stay open under an ever-increasing, invisible weight.

The next sound she heard was the newspaper thudding against the front door. Stevie stretched, inhaling the aromatic greeting of fresh-brewed coffee courtesy of the automatic timer on her coffee maker.

Rolling off the couch, Stevie looked at the gold and crystal coach clock on the wall and was surprised to find that she had slept for over three hours. *Mind over matter.* She gave her cheeks an encouraging pinch.

After coffee and the morning newspaper she would head for the health club that was part of her town-house community. A good strenuous workout would further banish Quintin Ward from her mind and her body.

Stevie enjoyed her three-times-a-week sessions with the various pieces of gym equipment and the aerobic dance class. Exercise made her feel better mentally and physically. It was a renewal of the

body that primed her spirit. She needed the prim-
ing more than ever today, not just to erase Quintin's memory, but to restore her business sense for
a video disk taping later in the afternoon.

She headed for the kitchen, needing the helping
hand of caffeine to get her started. Coffee mug in
hand, Stevie opened the front door a little and
reached out into the cold, hurriedly searching the
Astroturf-carpeted stoop for the newspaper. The
Tennesseean proved quite elusive.

Groaning, she wondered if the newspaper boy
had bounced it into her flower bed and smashed
her still-blooming poinsettias. She opened the door
wider and found—Quintin Ward.

He handed her the rolled morning paper, taking
from under his arm the evening edition. "I took
your advice and went out for coffee." His expression was bleak, his eyes lackluster. "I read last
night's *Banner*." Quintin pointed to a heavily inked
headline. "Awful article on teen-age suicide and
cults. If you fire Rob, I'm afraid he'll end up in an
airport lobby, wrapped in a sheet, with a shaved
head, selling flowers and shaking a tambourine."

4

~~~~~~~~~~~~~~~~~

Stevie gave the headline a cursory glance before taking both newspapers and tossing them in the direction of the foyer's console table. "How long have you been sitting on my doorstep?"

"I don't know." Quintin shrugged; his broad shoulders only succeeded in further bunching the tuxedo jacket. "An hour, maybe two."

She wrapped his icy, red chapped hands around her coffee-hot stoneware mug. "Why didn't you just go home?"

"I couldn't." His words were issued between greedy gulps of the steaming morning brew. "I owe you an apology."

The hazel eyes that studied Quintin's proud features mirrored Stevie's own ambivalent feelings.

Half of her wanted to accept the man's apology and then politely show him the door. The other half was being bombarded by a jumble of emotions, not the least of which was curiosity mixed with a perfectly silly but rather delicious feminine awareness.

Noting her prolonged hesitation, Quintin cleared his throat and held up one hand in a gesture of surrender. "No more confrontations—just communication. You're not what I thought."

She made her decision and waved him into the house's warm interior. "You mean I'm not *whom* you thought. The sins of the father." Stevie watched his knuckles whiten around the now empty cup.

He focused on the abstract metal sculpture that accented the hallway's white stucco wall. "I owe you an explanation as well as an apology." A muscle flexed in his lean cheek. "Perhaps that will make you understand why I've been acting so . . . so . . ."

"Insane," came her softly voiced encouragement.

His grin was lopsided. "I was going to say intolerant and rude."

Stevie pretended to ponder his addendum. "You're right"—her lashes lowered demurely—"that is a much more accurate description." She locked her arm through his. "Come along, Quintin Ward, an apology and an explanation are better delivered on a full stomach. You look like a man who could easily devour three slices of cinnamon French toast."

"Four," he corrected, and held out the empty mug, "plus more coffee."

Her low vibrant laugh eliminated the last vestiges of tension and wariness between them. Once in the kitchen Stevie repossessed the flower-strewn cup. She made a clucking noise as a peremptory finger tapped the newsprint stains on his hands. "The powder room is the second door on the right; washcloth and towels are in the linen closet."

Quintin smiled his thanks and ambled down the hall.

Under cover of the open refrigerator door, Stevie watched him walk away. The man said he felt uncomfortable in a tuxedo, but he certainly did the elegant garment just as much justice as he did his jeans! She fell victim to a totally foreign assault of giddiness that somehow had the strange effect of recharging and revitalizing her psyche.

She had never needed a man to define her, but Stevie readily acknowledged that there was an intangible something about Quintin Ward that excited her—mentally, emotionally and physically. With a sharp shake of her head she scolded herself for allowing these feelings to penetrate her reserve. Maybe her woman space had been too private for too long, so that she was grasping at anything and any man.

After all, Quintin was only interested in her because of his son. She was a liability rather than an asset; she was trouble rather than a blessing. *Let's face it, kiddo,* came her mental scold, *you are indigestion and the heartbreak of psoriasis rather than some enchanted evening!* Stevie exhaled an unladylike snort and reached for the milk, eggs and bread and hastily got down to the business of making breakfast.

From the doorway inquisitive masculine eyes quietly observed the domestic scene. Spatula in hand, his hostess seemed totally preoccupied with the contents of the electric fry pan. Quintin discovered he was engrossed not only with his problems but with Stephanie Brandt.

A self-condemning expression etched his features. When he was young he had acquired the macho habit of measuring women in inches and facial beauty. It was an adolescent error that had ultimately changed the direction of his life.

He had long outgrown his desire for a Barbie doll, seeking instead a mentally and emotionally put-together woman, one who knows where she's been and where she's going and what to do when she gets there.

These days he responded more to style and honesty; he was stimulated by a self-assured presence and a direct personality. And Quintin Ward was intensely aware that the woman who was making him breakfast had all of those virtues.

His first view of Stephanie Brandt had been in anger, and he had found nothing attractive about her features. Now Quintin's gaze tracked the early morning sun that slanted through the kitchen's east window to capture Stevie's silhouette in a soft, hazy beam of light.

The copper waves that teased her shoulders

were laced with veins of gold that alloyed them with the bronze piping on her ivory sleep shirt. Her irises were shards of a prism that became a barometer of her mood. Quintin had witnessed their transformation from a soft amber-brown to glittering green. He now found himself wondering what color they would be when she was sexually aroused.

A more intimate moment instantly came to mind as Quintin recalled the scene in his study. The remembered pressure from her soft, full lips and the taunting tip of her tongue percolated his blood. He could feel his body harden. Shifting in discomfort, Quintin diligently tried to terminate his masculine awareness but found that impossible as he watched the sinuous ripple of knee-length silk over her tall, lush female form.

Stevie's peripheral vision caught the movement of a shadow against the earth-toned linoleum. Her auburn head turned. "Perfect timing." She flashed a companionable smile. "Grab the coffee pot and follow me." She led Quintin into the adjoining dining room, where the large rectangular glass table was set for an intimate banquet for two.

"You didn't have to go to all this trouble." He glanced guiltily around the formal furnishings. The room was a glitter of glass, silver foil wallpaper and chrome wall etchings that was softened by peach carpeting, matching upholstered chairs, lacy hanging ferns and indoor palm trees. "The kitchen counter would have been fine." He quickly set the steaming coffee-filled decanter on a protective pad and pulled out her chair.

"Nonsense," she cheerfully dismissed his concern. "I thought you might appreciate a more relaxed atmosphere in which to—"

"Eat humble pie," came his wry summation.

Stevie made a fussy pretense of shaking out her napkin and placing it on her lap. "Your apology has already been accepted"—one tawny eyebrow arched in silent verification—"otherwise you wouldn't be sitting in that chair." An inscrutable expression masked her face. "However, I have a hunch a large slice of humility wouldn't hurt you any, Mr. Ward."

"Touché!" His tone was lighter. "Can we drop the formalities?" He moved his hand to cover hers; his thumb made a sweep along the inside of her wrist. "I'd much prefer talking to Stevie than Miss Brandt."

"And I'd prefer listening to Quintin." She was surprised to discover how cold and bereft her skin felt when he took his hand away. "Eat," Stevie ordered with a smile. She lifted the carafe, filled the oversize mugs with coffee and pulled the cream and sugar containers within easy reach.

"Delicious." His mouth may have been savoring the butter-drenched grilled French toast, but his gaze was absorbed in study of the lady on his left. "You have freckles!" Quintin's outspoken pronouncement caught them both off guard, and the room was filled with shared laughter.

"You've discovered my best-kept secret." Her lips puckered in an affected moue. "I usually keep these girlish sprinkles hidden by cosmetic wizardry," she related. "Freckles are hardly equated with a tough, professional image." Hesitating for a moment she added, "Or that of a siren."

He choked down a mouthful of coffee. "Ouch!" Quintin fumbled with the buttons on his dress shirt. "I really raked you over the coals, didn't I?"

Stevie nodded and continued to eat her breakfast.

"I suppose you'd like that explanation now?"

She studied the buttery squiggles her fork was drawing against the platinum-banded white china plate. "I am trusting you with my freckle secret." Stevie's low voice issued a sincere invitation.

Quintin opened his mouth to speak, then unexpectedly shoved a piece of toast into it. He turned inward, growing quiet and uneasy. The hair shirt he had worn for years had made him stronger and wiser. There were many things in his life he was proud of, and suddenly these were what he wanted to share with Stevie. Why further demean himself in her eyes by recounting a sordid past?

Strength and silence—weren't they the stuff of a real man? Never cry over the past, make an arrogant sweep of the present and march stalwartly into the future. Quintin stared off; a brief, rueful shadow crossed his face. He wondered if he hadn't become one-dimensional over the years. A dogmatic man who saw only black and white, yes and no, right and wrong. A cheap imitation of a real man.

The image of his son loomed large in his mind. Rob was the most important thing in his life, and maybe talking out his fears with a stranger would help him gain a new perspective.

Stranger—Stephanie Brandt? What was the fine line that turned a stranger into a friend and confidante? Was it time? Or was it—? His silent musings were interrupted by a feminine hand that covered his clenched fist. Quintin watched as she gently coaxed his hand to relax and then interlaced her slender fingers with his own.

When he finally spoke, he was heartened to hear that his voice gave no hint of his inner struggles. "The sins of the father. That quote is very apropos in this case, or at least I thought it was." His mouth twisted in a humorless smile.

"I was just eighteen months older than Rob when I fell under the spell of an older woman," Quintin continued. He found he lacked the courage to meet her eyes and focused instead on their entwined hands. "Andrea was the most stunning, fascinating, worldly creature any boy could ever imagine. Her makeup and dress were right out of *Vogue*, despite the fact that she was a secretary at the construction site I was working at during the summer.

"She held her own amid the dust, the concrete, the foul language and the wolf whistles. She was cool and aloof and I was in love. This was no giggling high school girl who teased and tormented in the backseat of a car. Andrea was a woman who knew everything. I wanted that knowledge. I wanted her."

He paused to let a swallow of coffee ease a dry throat. "She was amused with the fresh flower I put on her desk every day, perhaps even flattered by my solicitous attention. I still wonder whatever made her accept my invitation to dinner. Maybe she thought she'd get a laugh and a free meal.

"But neither one of us ever laughed and the meal was the first of many. My attraction for her was reciprocated. I was young in years but mature in looks and attitude. Our affair was very intense; our casual dates quickly became intimate and Andrea quickly became pregnant."

Quintin heard Stevie's sharp intake of breath and felt the corresponding increase of pressure on his hand. "I was stunned and angry. She was eight years older and no virgin. I wrongly assumed she was taking precautions.

"Andrea had other ideas. She knew I was making good money and she hated working, so she hatched this foolproof plan—never telling me until she was well into her third month." He took a deep breath. "We got married and Rob arrived six months later.

"Andrea was never meant to be a mother. The baby ruined her health and destroyed her figure. He cried all night, so she couldn't sleep. She felt stifled and confined. Our apartment was small to begin with and grew even smaller when a crib and assorted baby items were added.

"I suppose I wasn't much help. I worked days on the construction site and went to school at night, hoping to get ahead. An exhausted, bookworm husband was not Andrea's idea of fun. We fought all the time.

"She hated me. I hated her. Poor Rob was horribly neglected. Seven months later Andrea walked out. I got the baby, a stack of bills and divorce papers. She hasn't seen or ever attempted to make contact with Rob. I don't even know if she's alive, and frankly I don't care."

Stevie hesitated a moment. "Quint, how did you ever manage?"

"Exactly the same way other single parents manage"—his dark head rested against the chair's peach upholstered back—"one day at a time. My engineering studies were put on hold. I took a job as a land surveyor and took Rob with me on my assignments. It worked for a while, but the expenses kept mounting up. I had to get a full-time job and leave the baby with a sitter."

His free hand wiped the sweat from his forehead. "Those were lost years, Stevie. I can't even remember them." Quintin's voice registered amazement. "What I do remember is missing my son's first steps, hearing him call the sitter's husband 'Da-da' and feeling both guilty and resentful every time I looked at him. Hell, I was only in my twenties and fed up with being responsible for everything and everyone. Sometimes I . . . I . . ." He groped for the right words and failed to find them.

For the first time since he started speaking, Quintin focused on Stevie. He wondered what he would see—pity, condemnation or revulsion. But her eyes were soft amber brown, and they held respect, admiration and understanding. That, coupled with the continued pressure from her hand, gave him the courage to continue.

"Things were easier once Rob started school. I was even able to resume my engineering studies. Eventually I got my degree and, with a little money and a lot of bravado, I took over a bankrupt construction company and slowly brought it back into the world of profit.

"I became obsessed with work and the almighty dollar. I wanted to get 'there' yesterday and I was never quite sure where 'there' was. I felt cheated out of so much and envious of my crew's free-wheeling life-style. I was bitter and surly and so very angry."

Quintin gave a rueful laugh. "What really scared me was that one day I turned around and discovered my baby son was full grown. He was a teen-ager on the threshold of becoming a man.

"We were both older. Rob was savoring his coming of age, while I was cursing time. I was again consumed with guilt and tried to recover all the lost years, to give my son all the things he had missed.

"I had always wanted Rob to have a house with a backyard, so I bought Cedar Hill and together we built ourselves a home. I was after this great one-to-one relationship with my son, more friend and pal than parent. I had this secret dream that he would emulate me, become an engineer or perhaps an architect, and we'd be partners. But Rob wasn't that interested in construction; he was fascinated with music and—"

"And that's when I came in," Stevie adjoined. "The older woman, the florist's bill for a fresh rose every day. It's no wonder you thought—"

His right hand clamped solidly over hers, sandwiching it between both of his. "I incorrectly assumed that history was repeating itself." Brown eyes stared into hazel. "Stevie, I'm sorry. I—"

Her fingers stilled his lips. "I'll say this just one more time: You've been forgiven." She was thoughtful for a long moment. "Quintin, I still think I should fire Rob on Monday. Out of sight, out of mind," came her offer. "Oh, Rob may brood and become sullen, but—" She pursed her lips. "Now, why are you shaking your head?"

"Because you don't understand the teen-age mind," he argued. "Kids don't crawl into corners and sulk. They view everything as a punishment. They run away and end up working the streets or joining cults or committing suicide. One boy killed himself because he had his TV taken away!"

"You're letting that newspaper article undermine your common sense," she was quick to protest. "Rob's a good, decent kid who knows right from wrong. You've given him the best upbringing. He's not going to turn into . . . into a juvenile delinquent over me."

"That's probably what my parents thought," came Quintin's abrupt rejoinder. "I was Rob. I've been in his position. My folks kept telling me that I had my whole future ahead of me; I was making a fool of myself with Andrea; she was too old for me and I didn't know what love was. Did I listen? No."

His fist slammed against his thigh. "I was stubborn and headstrong and knew everything. The more they talked against her, the more fiercely I protected her; the more they pointed out all the bad, the more good I saw. I moved out. They disowned me the day I married her. And Rob . . . well, he suffered again. It was a long, long time before my parents and I were able to get back together.

"Rob is his father's son." Quintin sighed, the grooves in his lean cheeks deepening under stress. "He was very vocal last night in his protection of you."

Stevie winced. "All right. I won't fire him." She rubbed her nose while she did some further consideration. "He's misinterpreted the atmosphere of my office," she explained. "While I run a very tight, strict ship, everyone is exceptionally friendly and relaxed." Her eyes widened. "How about if I start being more sharp and curt, perhaps even rude? No more freebees, records, tickets. Nothing. I can try to arrange my calendar so I'm out of the office the afternoons Rob works, and when I am there, he'll find me more the Iron Maiden." She gave Quintin a hopeful smile.

His knuckle stroked the soft curve of her cheekbone. "Iron Maiden?" Both his eyes and his voice registered doubt.

"I can be vicious," came her stout affirmation.

"I bet you can." His tone was soft and not at all mocking. "But if you make such a sudden change, Stevie, Rob would probably accuse me of turning you against him, and then who knows what he'd do." Quintin shook his head. "Rob is in love with you. He's living in this storybook dreamworld, where you're the fair princess and he's the handsome prince on the white charger who sweeps you off your feet and carries you away to—"

"A gingerbread castle covered with candy," she mumbled, pushing her empty plate to one side. Elbows on the table, Stevie rested her chin in her hands; three vertical lines furrowed her smooth forehead. "How about talking to a psychologist or the high school guidance counselor? Or—" She gave a little scream when his open palm hit the top of the glass table.

"Sorry, but you just gave me the most brilliant idea."

"I . . . I did?"

"Yes"—Quintin grabbed her shoulders—"when you mentioned candy!" He laughed at her wide-eyed blank expression. "What happens when someone eats too much candy?"

"They break out and gain ten pounds," came Stevie's sullen response.

"They get sick," he corrected. "Sick to the point of nausea, so sick they never want to see candy again."

She nodded in mute agreement, eyes narrowing in contemplation of Quintin's ever-broadening grin.

"*You* are going to be Rob's candy," he announced, his index finger pushing up her dropped jaw. "We are going to cram Stephanie Brandt down his throat until the mention of your name makes him physically ill."

"Gee, thanks a lot!" Twisting her shoulder free, Stevie slumped down in the chair. "That's a stupid idea."

"It's brilliant." Quintin sat back, arms folded across his chest. "If I told Rob he couldn't have you, he'd want you . . . so I'll tell him to go for it. I'll tell him to treat you just like any other date, and if it's true love, the age difference won't matter."

"Stupid, stupid, stupid." Each word was repeated more loudly and firmly than the last.

"Nonsense. It's perfect. Rob will see how out of place you are in the high school world. His friends will tease the hell out of him, and you know how effective peer group pressure is. All you have to do is act bored and say how childish everything is."

"I will be bored and this is childish." Abruptly Stevie squared her shoulders and assumed her most intimidating business stare. "Quintin, I am the president of a corporation. I do not have time for this idiocy." She made herself sound as vicious as possible. "Why don't you just turn the kid over your knee and paddle some sense into him? I'll even hold him down," she offered with a smile.

"Stevie, please. This will work, believe me. Reverse psychology. Let them have what they want and then they don't want it."

"But I hated being a teen-ager, and going through high school the first time was tragic enough! No. Never. No. . . ." Stevie discovered her biggest mistake was looking at Quintin. His eyes were wide chestnut pools that tugged at her heart, and his silently mouthed pleas proved to be her final undoing. "Damn! All right. I'll go along with this"—she pointed an accusing finger—"but only for a while, and it had better work and work fast."

"This is a very well calculated risk." Quintin rubbed his hands with glee. "My plan is foolproof."

"So why do I feel like the fool?" Stevie grumbled.

"I'm going home and start the ball rolling." He stood up and lifted his jacket from the back of the chair. "When Rob comes to work on Monday, you just act the part of a woman in love."

Stevie trailed after him to the door. "I'll . . . I'll try."

Quintin heard the reluctance in her voice and observed the dejected slump of her posture. His hands cupped her face; thumbs gently tracing the curve along her cheekbones. "Just cover up those freckles and add a healthy splash of that perfume you were wearing last night."

His admission piqued her vanity. "You mean my perfume actually made an impression?" She moved closer; her bare feet stepped between his shoes. Through a fringe of black lashes she gauged the subtle change in Quintin. The puritanical father was now a responsive male.

Virile hands followed the supple curve of her neck before sliding around her tapered back; the fluid ivory silk moved against the calloused roughness of his fingers. "On my personal Richter scale of one to ten"—Quintin's voice deepened; his eyes concentrated on Stevie's half-parted lips—"you registered a twenty. And this is so you'll know what *I* call a kiss."

His mouth took leisurely possession of hers. The firm masculine lips were compelling and purposeful as they stroked the satiny fullness of their feminine counterpart. His inquisitive tongue probed into the lush recesses beyond, trespassing to savor her sweetness.

The heat of Quintin's body burned into Stevie. Her skin felt hot and tingling, shot through with delicious sensations that made her tremble against his lean frame. Her hands made fluttering motions in the air; her fingers anchored into his wide leather belt, seeking support. Blood effervesced in her veins. Stevie felt as if she had drunk a magnum of champagne.

When Quintin finally released her, they were both breathing hard. "You're right," Stevie acknowledged at length, her right hand twisting the brass knob. "You do know how to kiss." She gave him a little shove into the brisk morning air.

The blinking red light on the telephone alerted Stevie to the phone call. Pulling headphones from her ears, she lifted the receiver and heard Quintin's voice. "I'm just calling with a progress report and to make sure you're not getting cold feet about tomorrow."

Uncurling her legs, she contemplated her wiggling poppy-red toenails. "More than my feet are cold," she groused. "Quintin, I don't like deceiving Rob. I don't like deceiving anyone."

"This is not a matter of deception," he countered quickly, his tone low and soothing. "We are actually saving him from reacting impulsively and ruining his whole life." Quintin cleared his throat. "Rob and I had quite a civil chat about you last night. My compliance surprised him, but at least the father-son lines of communication are still open."

She sniffed and sighed. "I'm glad about that."

"Tomorrow afternoon, just do your womanly duty and seduce my son."

"That's easier said than done," came her caustic retort. "I haven't got the faintest idea how to seduce a seventeen-year-old child."

"I know just the thing to get you in the mood," he announced. "An orgy." He laughed at her strangled reply and added, "I'll be there in half an hour."

By the time the door chimes heralded Quintin's arrival, Stevie had whipped herself into a fine rage. Her greeting echoed the Sunday night weather: frigid and frosty. "You've really got crust, Quintin Ward. I thought we—"

"No, *this* has crust, Miss Brandt." He tapped the large white cardboard box. Brown eyes were alight with laughter at her disapproving expression. "Pepperoni, wasn't it?" Quintin chucked her under the chin. "You're right, you do look as good in fleece as you did in silk," he added, viewing with appreciation the floor-length gray sweatshirt lounger that draped her well-curved figure in soft sweaterlike folds.

"My, my, but you are in good humor!" Stevie found it impossible to halt the smile that curved her lips. She motioned him inside. "Are things that much improved between you and Rob?"

"Let's just say that I felt confident enough that when he said he was going to the movies with a few buddies and then stopping for burgers at the video arcade, I believed him." He followed her into the living room. "Yesterday I would have suspected him of planning to run away." Quintin tried to sound offhanded with his next question. "I called you a couple of times yesterday but kept getting your answering machine."

"Were you the seven clicks?" She relocated the red amaryllis dish garden from the cocktail table to the end table and took possession of the aromatic carton. "I was at the studio, monitoring a video disk taping that lasted well into this morning." Her auburn head nodded toward the plum lacquered wall unit, where the television was broadcasting video but not audio. "There's the finished product."

Quintin squinted at the five musicians who gyrated amid spectacular lighting and fireworks displays. "I love the lack of sound, but I think your color is slightly off."

"No, the Pit Stops do have green hair."

He sighed and pulled a wad of napkins from the pocket of his tan corduroy shirt-jacket. "Isn't there a group that looks perfectly normal?"

"We do have a few," she said, laughing, as they settled cross-legged on the carpet, the low glass table adding Chinese ambience to their Italian meal. "The Pit Stops are a very talented group. Their first single went platinum and their new album gold after sixty days. The green-striped hair is their new punk look." She handed Quintin a slice of pizza. "They're a young group; the oldest is twenty, and they're impatient. They want to have a record in all the categories at the same time. So yesterday they made their first sojourn into new wave."

His long denim-clad legs stretched more comfortably beneath the table. "You sound as though you disagreed with that decision."

Stevie picked at a slice of pepperoni that was caught in a cloak of creamy mozzarella cheese. "Let's just say I wasn't thrilled. The Pit Stops' original sound was a mix of rock 'n' roll and blues that went over big. They did a concert tour last month that got rave reviews from the critics and was recorded for HBO.

"We had a strategy meeting Friday morning to show them that the change would be more con than pro. The more we resisted, the more the group insisted. I don't know. The record industry is so changeable; what's 'in' today is 'out' by tomorrow. So I guess we just wait and see." Her teeth sank into the thick crust, the rich tomato sauce exciting her taste buds.

Quintin looked triumphant. "You just proved my point," he told her. "You said no and they said yes.

Same with Rob. Once I approved his interest in you, he just sat there speechless and blinking."

Her nose wrinkled. "I hope you're right. Forfeiting a few bucks on a record is quite different from losing the trust of your son. I don't want anything to jeopardize your relationship with Rob."

"Your saying that means a lot. Don't worry, nothing is going to happen." Quintin smiled and reached for another slice of pizza. "My plan is brilliant!"

"Famous last words!" Stevie plucked the string of mozzarella that looped from his mouth to his pizza. "I'll get some wine." Her finger pointed into the box. "Don't touch that piece right there."

"Have you thought about your plan of attack for tomorrow?" he called, pilfering an extra slice of the zesty sausage and trying to rearrange the others so she wouldn't notice the indentation in the cheese.

"No, I haven't." She returned carrying a glass of burgundy in each hand. "You're the man with all the brilliant ideas." Stevie's tone and manner were nonchalant. "What would you suggest I do?"

After carefully setting the crystal goblets on the table, his fingers circled her wrists, pulling her down on her knees. "I suppose I could give you a few pointers." Quintin manufactured a sigh, his dark eyes taking on a lustrous sheen. "This is purely in the interest of furthering your education, of course."

"Purely," came her satiny rejoinder.

"You have to be subtle," he instructed. His fingers laced amid the auburn richness that swirled to her shoulders. "Take things slow and easy." He glimpsed the tender curve of her ear through the fiery tendrils. "Never scare."

Quintin leaned close. "This is always nice." His warm breath caressed her ear.

"Hmmm." Closing her eyes, Stevie willingly succumbed to the sweet sensations he was producing.

"And this." His tongue made a teasing exploration of the curves and hollows and played with the tiny gold loop that accented the lobe. Despite the volume of fabric that cloaked Stevie's body, Quintin's hands discovered the rounded symmetry of her female form.

"Perhaps even this." His teeth nipped a gentle bite into the tender skin below her ear. The mysterious blend that was her perfume tantalized his senses. "Of course, the problem with all this," Quintin whispered, his dark head nuzzling the juncture of her neck and shoulder, "is that you're making it very difficult for me to sit still."

He pulled her more fully into his arms, letting his dark gaze savor every aspect of her flushed features. "Despite all my fears about Rob"—Quintin's hand settled possessively in the curve of her waist—"I'd dearly love to thank him for introducing me to you."

At the mention of his son, Stevie's expression turned sober, her pliant form becoming more rigid. "I really like Rob. I'm afraid all this is going to boomerang and he'll end up hurting." Even, white teeth snagged at her lower lip. "It's a terrible thing to discover the person you love has been lying."

His left hand warmly cupped the side of her neck, his thumb caressing the velvety line of her jaw. "Will you tell me about it?" Quintin's voice was low and compelling.

Stevie briefly wondered about sharing her past with Quintin but discovered an urgent need to know his reaction. "You're not the only one who's ever made the mistake of loving the wrong person," she recounted, her tone slightly bitter. "I was engaged to a very cunning man. Paul not only fooled me but my parents as well.

"He was charming and attentive and very romantic." Her fingers straightened the high collar on Quintin's turtleneck, her palm taking comfort in the sinewy strength beneath the beige sweater. "While I was mature and sensible when it came to business and higher learning, I was a very naive twenty-three when it came to men.

"I fell very quickly under Paul's spell, perhaps more girlishly in love with the romance he provided than the man himself. My days were spent planning the perfect June garden wedding; Paul's days were spent planning to take over as head of my father's business. What better way than to marry the boss's daughter!

"He played up to my parents, especially my dad, becoming the son Steven Brandt had never had. But when Paul found out that the presidency of the company was still to be mine, all his avowed declarations of love splintered during a blazing fight."

Stevie was silent for a moment, and despite the ensuing seven years she could still vividly remember how hurt and used and unclean she had felt. "It made this lady very, very cautious," she added finally, and moved to slide off Quintin's lap.

His hands hindered her departure. "Speaking from a purely selfish viewpoint"—he turned her face toward his—"I'm glad you've been cautious." He spoke against her lips. "Very, very glad."

She exhaled a musical sigh. "I seem to have thrown caution to the wind where you're concerned, Mr. Ward," came her tart rebuke. "But it's Rob that I'm worried about, and his reactions and feelings and—"

"I respect your fears," he interrupted, his fingers combing amid the silky depths of her hair, "but I'm positive everything is going to work out perfectly."

Stevie reached for the wineglasses, handed him one; the crystal clicked together in a mutual toast. "I guess we'll know tomorrow!"

5

~~~~~~~~~~~

Rob came home whistling." Quintin's tone was harsh. *"He* smiled all the way up the stairs to finish his homework." The front door of Stevie's town house was fiercely slammed shut.

Feeling the reverberation in her head, Stevie winced and emitted a low groan. "No noise." The washcloth that was pressed against her forehead was opened and placed over her entire face. "Whisper. I have a Pac-Man headache."

Quintin lifted the navy terrycloth and breathed in sharply with disgust after viewing her blanched, pinched features. "This is the way Rob was supposed to look, not you." His arms formed a comforting belt that encircled her waist. "What happened, Stevie?"

"Health food and Astro Smash." Her lips mumbled the cryptic explanation into the open V-neck of his burgundy pullover. The woodsy masculine cologne that clung to his skin proved to be the perfect panacea for her frazzled nerves. "What's the matter with teen-agers today? Don't they eat good, greasy junk food and listen to the jukebox anymore?"

He half-carried, half-dragged her weary body onto the comfortable confines of the living room's velvet pit group. "Give me a blow-by-blow."

"Please, that's exactly what's going on in my head and stomach."

Quintin made appropriate clucking noises while he guided Stevie's throbbing head into position across his gray-tweed-covered thighs. "You poor baby." He replaced the damp compress.

Stevie sighed her pleasure during the soothing massage that was bestowed on her forehead and temples. "You would have been proud of me, Quint," she said at length. "I was subtle but provocative. Robbie stuttered and stammered over issuing the dinner invitation, and when I said yes, he walked into the door frame and dropped the outgoing-mail basket.

"At six o'clock I wedged my body into the front seat of his VW and we were off." One hazel eye opened to level an accusing stare. "You could have fixed the car's heater and replaced the glass in the passenger's side window. The wind really whips right through that cardboard."

Masculine fingertips tenderly closed her eyelid. "Why do you think Rob needed an after-school job? That damn car is forever undergoing major reconstructive surgery!"

"That is little consolation to a woman with an earache!" She felt his ministering fingers roam to the spot in question. "Hmmmm."

"Where did you have dinner?"

"Rob took me to the Bountiful Harvest." Her eye opened again. "I do not call tofu and lettuce covered with fuzzy bean sprouts and wheat germ plus a glass of yeast-laden papaya juice dinner."

Quintin snickered. "What do you call it?"

"Physical cruelty," came her sharp retort. With both eyes open Stevie turned her head and let an impertinent index finger press into his flat stomach. "I doubt if you subsist on rabbit food, Mr. Ward; more like steak and potatoes?"

An indentation formed in Quintin's right cheek. "Rare and one inch thick, with a baked potato dripping with melted butter and sour cream and sprinkled with chives."

The tip of her tongue poked a silent comment. "That's mental cruelty; you could have lied." She groaned again and closed her eyes. "I have a tummyache. My digestive tract doesn't know what to do with healthy food; it's been thoroughly corrupted by years of such perverse pleasures as pizza and hot-fudge sundaes and tacos and fried chicken."

His thumb traced the oval curve of her jaw down her throat to blaze a sinuous trail through the valley of her breasts; his large palm conformed to the rounded contours of her stomach. "Feel better?"

The erotic warmth of his hand quickly permeated her oatmeal sweater dress. Her body blossomed under his touch, overtly and without shame. Voluptuous ripples of pleasure washed over her, making the sensitive nipples of her breasts peak beneath their lacy brassiere prison. "You've got a wonderful healing touch."

Quintin's index finger outlined her full lips. "You should sample my bedside manner." His silky, resonant voice revealed his own undisguised desire.

The black pupils of her eyes were ringed by narrow amber bands. "I'll keep your invitation in mind," came her sultry promise. For a long moment Stevie indulged herself by mapping the virile contours of Quintin's face. His blunt jaw and chiseled features had a very unsettling effect on her usually stoic emotions.

Abruptly she closed her eyes and determinedly refocused her attention on the subject of his son. Stevie cleared her throat and continued. "After feasting on that magnificent vitamin-enriched dinner, Robbie took me to Wizard's Arcade. Video games surrounded me. Everything beebeed and whizzed, zapped and kappowed, exploded and crashed or played cute little tunes that signified something big was eating something small." She shuddered in remembrance.

"I've worked with sound all my life," she grumbled to Quintin, "but that place charted new decibel levels." Her fingers coaxed his to massage a spot above the bridge of her nose. "Kids say those machines improve their reflexes and their eye-to-hand coordination, but you couldn't prove it by me.

"There are no instructions on any of the games, Quint. And all those moving colors and sounds just made me nervous and frustrated. Submariner's Revenge gobbled up four tokens and I only scored twenty points. Donkey Kong was a complete wipe-out, and I'll bet anything I'm going to have nightmares about the ghosts of Pac-Man chasing me, and— Quintin! Stop that laughing," Stevie ordered.

Grabbing his shoulders, she struggled into a sitting position on his lap. "Actually I don't understand how Rob could have come home happy. I was a terrible date."

He turned his laughter into a cough and valiantly tried to compose himself. "Just how were you so terrible?" Quintin smoothed her auburn hair.

Stevie ticked off her faults as a date on her fingers. "First, I kept up a running complaint about his car's lack of virtue; second, I acted like a little kid eating liver when we had our health food salads; third, I corrected ninety-nine percent of his grammar every time he opened his mouth; fourth, I looked more like his mother than his date in this dress and towered over him in my high heels; and fifth, I kept running through his tokens at the arcade." A proud smile curved her lips. "When Rob wakes up tomorrow, he'll be taking my name in vain over his cornflakes."

"Granola and bran," Quintin corrected, a companionable grin slanting his lips. "You've made me feel three hundred percent better," he confessed. As his hand moved to cup her chin, the digital display on his platinum watch caught his attention. "Damn"—he frowned at the hour—"I've got to leave. I told Rob I was going to the market."

Stevie slid off his legs and straightened her dress while she followed him to the entrance hall. "The more I think about it, Quint, the more I'm convinced that one date with me was probably more than enough." Her eyes were wide and her expression serious. "Poor Rob probably expected a torrid, steamy evening of rapture, and I emptied the kid's wallet in three hours and didn't even give him a good-night kiss!"

"How about if I take one." It was a statement rather than a question, and Quintin realized that he had been subconsciously planning this possibility all day and had dreamed about it all the night before.

His hands cupped her face, his fingers spread amid silken hair that spilled copper fire over his wrists. Stevie's lips were soft and yielding on his and willingly accepted the intrusion of his anxious tongue. He took sustenance from her, his own energies seemingly refueled by merging with hers.

The taste of him was the antidote for Stevie's enervated emotions. She savored this vital connection, sharing the moment as they shared each other. Her body spoke a silent language to his, and where they touched—at the shoulders, the hips and the thighs—they seemed electrified.

With obvious reluctance Quintin relinquished her mouth. His fingertips stroked the subtle hollow beneath her cheekbones. "I'll call you tomorrow."

Stevie leaned against the locked front door, letting the solid oak brace her decidedly languid bones while she took two deep breaths. A secret part of her had stopped wondering and started hoping. She found she desperately wanted this problem with Rob solved so her relationship with Quintin could continue to progress.

"You're going to win the florist's award for most roses received in a month." Gloria Lansing's dulcet announcement greeted her boss as Stevie opened the glass reception-room doors. "Bobby Ward left a single red rose and this note on his way to school."

"Damn!" Stevie's gray leather attaché case bounced onto the blue carpet. "I was absolutely positive that last night's encounter would kill the attraction," she grumbled, and reluctantly accepted the proffered white envelope. "Oh, God, listen to this: 'I know how busy you are, but will you come with me to the basketball game Friday night?' "

Gloria failed to hide her amusement. "Looks like the son checkmated his father's reverse psychology."

Stevie released the three buttons on her brown wool gabardine jacket and slid her hand into the pocket of the matching skirt. "No, no, I think Quintin's idea is right. In fact Dear Abby said something to the same effect in her column this morning. And you'll notice our next date coincides with his paycheck."

Her nose wrinkled at the hastily scrawled note. "I hate basketball. Give me a seat on the fifty-yard line, a blanket and a thermos of brandy-laced coffee and I'm happy."

She tapped her chin with the invitation. "Maybe I just didn't come across as strong as I thought." Stevie's eyes widened under a sudden inspiration. "What's de rigueur for high school gymnasium wear these days?"

Her secretary looked intrigued. "Still preppie. Jeans and an alligator shirt."

"Wouldn't Bobby be embarrassed if his date shows up in a silk dress and heels?"

"Won't you be embarrassed climbing the bleachers in your silk dress and twisting your ankle in your heels?" Gloria made the wry prediction.

Stevie's lips curved. "Forgot about that." Mauve-tinted fingernails made random zigzags along the roll collar of her ivory blouse. "Well, I could still overdress," she insisted. "Remember that rambunctious raccoon vest with the hanging tails Cowboy 'Wild Bill' Crocker brought me from his Rocky Mountain tour?" Tawny brows arched in renewed enthusiasm.

Gloria laughed and nodded. "Do I ever! We almost bought a cage and food for the darn thing."

"What if I team that vest with suede pants tucked into those armadillo-skin cowboy boots that were another present? I'd say Bobby Ward would be one red-faced boy over his *ne plus ultra* date!" She bent to retrieve her fallen briefcase. "Dig that stuff out of the prop room for me, would you, Gloria. I'd better give Quintin a call and—"

"You won't have to. He's been lighting up the switchboard every five minutes." Gloria tapped her watch. "You've got just two more minutes to wait," she promised, and pulled a pencil from her gray topknot. "I'm going to have to rearrange your Friday-night schedule. Luckily I've made your entire calendar erasable."

"Thank you, Mother," Stevie cracked wise. "What's on for the next few days?" She inspected the neatly typed sheet Gloria handed her. "Ouch. I am busy. Do the best you can with Friday; see what you can shove on to Saturday. Until this nonsense gets—"

Gloria grinned as the telephone beep interrupted. "There's the guy with the cute tush." She winked, lifted the receiver and intoned: "Good morning, Brandt Associates. One moment, please." She pressed the hold button. "It's him. You've got five minutes before you meet with RCA Records," she called to the redhead's sprinting figure.

Stevie answered with a breathless "Hello."

"You weren't as terrible a date as you thought," Quintin's deep voice grumbled across the line. "I assume you already received the flower and the basketball invitation."

Her hip wiggled into a comfortable position on

the edge of the oak desk. "They were here when I arrived. But I came up with something for Friday that should dampen Bobby's spirits."

"Tell me."

"Let us just say I will not be dressed like the all-American high school girl when I go to the gym."

Her melodic laugh revived his spirits. "How about if I drop by tonight and you can model your outfit for me?"

"I'd like nothing better," she admitted. Her hand tightened around the brown receiver as her gaze focused on the scheduling sheet in her left hand. "But I have a client who's been with this company for twenty years flying in from the coast. Normally my dad would come out of retirement and play host, but my folks are on vacation in Hawaii."

Mentally she tried to break some appointments but found it impossible. "Quintin, I'm booked solid. My secretary is scrambling now to rearrange my calendar so I can attend the basketball game. This is the music industry's busy time," Stevie informed him. "There are wall-to-wall award shows, tour dates and recording sessions to book, and contracts are up for renewal. I may only see home to shower and change clothes."

"This is my slow time," came his rueful declaration. "Construction literally halts in the winter. I've got a few bids to work up, but most of my crew is on vacation." Quintin paused for a second, then added, "How about if I wait at your place Friday night?"

"Sounds perfect." Stevie nodded as Gloria stuck her head around the half-open door and nodded toward the grandmother clock in the corner, which silently indicated the time. "I've got to go. There's an extra front-door key taped to the bottom of the flower planter."

"Did you use too much blusher this morning or is that your natural reaction to Papa Ward?"

Stevie's thumb stroked the smooth cat's-eye gemstone that was on the ring finger of her right hand. "It's my natural reaction to Quintin Ward," she answered, rubbing the ring as if it were a worry bead.

"So why the frown?"

Preoccupied hazel eyes looked at the woman who was more confidante–second mother than employee. "Here in the office I'm more masculine than feminine. I'm assertive, judgmental and decisive. When I'm with Quintin, I turn into . . ." Stevie groped for the right words. ". . . into a stereotypical female: shy, nervous, submissive. I enjoy being independent, but I find I don't mind leaning on him and letting him do all the thinking." Stevie shrugged. "What do you make of that?"

"I think you should trust your internal cues." Gloria smiled. "A smart woman knows how to combine independence and intimacy." She jerked a thumb toward the clock. "And right now you are scheduled to be—"

"One tough broad." Stevie winked, straightened her jacket and headed for the door.

* * *

Stevie struggled out of the rust-spangled red Volkswagen amid a chorus of gleeful good nights and used the last of her energy to wave. The twenty-six steps to her front door were the most painful she had ever taken. The last ten were finished walking on the heels of her boots.

Quintin had the door opened before she even rang the bell. "I was peeking out the front window; it looks like you were well chaperoned."

"Eight." She waddled past him into the foyer. "Eight people in that little car." Stevie motioned for him to help her out of the raccoon vest. "I got to sit between the two front seats, wedged behind the stick shift and on the lap of a kid who kept belching." She piled a seemingly endless number of black-ringed fur tails on the foyer's glass and chrome console.

In the dimly lit living room Stevie spied a bottle of wine and two glasses waiting on the cocktail table. "Oh, Quintin, that was sweet." She turned and smiled. "I've got to sit down and take off these boots. In the middle of the second half my toes went numb." Stevie bent over and pressed her fingers into the leather. "They're dead, Quint, or at the very least gangrenous."

"Stevie, you can't sit down." His words sounded strangled.

"Why not?"

"You've got . . . uhh . . . a big wad of Dubble Bubble on the seat of your pants."

"Quintin, please . . ." she begged, and looked

between her legs at his upside-down image. "Please tell me you're joking."

He stared at the gooey mound that was a conspicuous pink ornament on the loden suede. "I'm sorry."

Stevie rested her head against the stucco wall. "These pants are brand new." She groaned. "They cost a fortune."

Quintin brushed back an auburn wave that curtained her face. "Let me have an ice cube and a butter knife and I'll make them good as new," he promised, "but first let's get rid of those boots."

Straddling each leg in turn, he forcefully but carefully eased off the pointed vamp of the garishly designed footwear. "These damn things are obscene," Quintin scolded as he gently removed Stevie's socks. He cursed again viewing her red, blistered toes and heels.

"I thought so." She moaned in relief. "Rob thought they were 'like totally total,'" she mimicked, "and one of his friends, Jack, the kid wearing the camouflage coordinates, told me I was 'like tubular.' Tubular!" A hiss was issued between clenched teeth.

"That's a compliment," he translated with a chuckle. Quintin's hands flowed along the sides of her torso, examining the lithe curves beneath her thin sand-colored sweater. "No one could ever accuse your body of resembling a tube."

"Right now this body is one big muscle spasm. My ninety-year-old grandmother doesn't have this many aches and pains," she muttered, letting Quintin take her by the hand into the kitchen. "Eight people packed like . . . like sardines in that little car. I know I've slipped a disk."

"How did your date become a group effort?"

Leaning over the counter, Stevie propped her elbows on the butcher-block top. "I don't know," she sighed. "We drew them like flies. One came to borrow money and stayed; another helped himself to our popcorn; three others needed rides home; and one kid kept tickling himself with the raccoon tails." She shuddered, then shivered again as the ice cube Quintin was holding wet through her pants and made frigid contact with her skin.

As his palm clamped the ice tightly on the chewing gum, his fingers shaped the rounded contour of her right buttock. "I gather your outrageous outfit wasn't so avant-garde." Quintin reclined close against her side.

She made a face. "Let's just say I was the only one embarrassed. Although someone did ask me if I was wearing an endangered species." Stevie gave his arm a light swat when he laughed. "The truth is *I* was the endangered species," she snapped crossly. "Nobody speaks the King's English anymore. The word *like* prefaces everything. I swear, it has to be rated among the most annoying four-letter words of this century."

His eyes radiated the same tenderness as his voice. "You had a terrible night."

"I certainly did," Stevie concurred, her mouth puckered as if to cry. "There must have been a million kids swarming in that gymnasium. Quintin, do you know what a million sweaty kids smell like!" She shuddered again. "They screamed when their team had the ball; they screamed when the other team had the ball. The cheerleaders screamed all the time. Some idiot kept blowing 'Charge!' on his trumpet.

"At halftime the band was loud and off-key. My hot dog was cold and the bun dotted with mold. I've got soda and mustard on my sweater and bubble gum on my—" Her weary barrage was abruptly terminated by Quintin's mouth. Firm yet gentle, provocative yet soothing, his lips made a much more pleasant finish.

As if loath to break contact entirely, he rested his forehead against hers. "You weren't supposed to be the one getting the short end of the deal."

"Speaking of ends, mine's awfully cold."

Quintin threw back his head and laughed. "Okay, okay, that should be long enough." He tossed what was left of the ice cube into the sink. "Have I told you how much I missed not seeing you these past three days?"

Stevie twisted around to watch him rummage in the cutlery drawer. The red plaid flannel shirt emphasized his muscular physique, the navy cords his slim hips. She had heard many times that silly line about a heart turning over but never understood what it meant until right now. "How much did you miss me?" Her voice was low and unconsciously seductive.

His expression was serious; his eyes focused

steadily on her. "Even more than I thought now that I'm near you." Quintin scrutinized her features; the softly flushed cheeks couldn't hide the dullness in her hazel eyes. "You're working too hard." He brandished the butter knife in a warning gesture.

"It's been a long week, and for me it's still not over." She could feel the dull blade scrape her pants. "I've got three prospective clients doing demo tapes tomorrow, and I'm having a Sunday brunch meeting with those LA people I told you about."

The gum-coated utensil was tossed on the counter. "Good as new," Quintin announced, giving her derriere a pat. He moved behind her; his arms wrapped around her waist; his body molded itself across her still-bent form. "Can you possibly fit me into your busy schedule . . ." His warm breath tickled her ear. ". . . say, lunch on Monday."

"As long as you don't take me anyplace that serves health food or cold hot dogs or has video games."

"Soft music, candle lanterns and Chinese," came his husky promise. "A lunch for mature audiences only." Quintin rubbed his cheek against the red-gold wealth of her hair; the mysterious nuance of her perfume held him captive.

"Hmmm. That sounds heavenly. I'll be ready at twelve-thirty." When Stevie attempted to turn more fully into his arms, a sharp cramp stabbed into her back. "Ohhh, Quintin, if you pick me up in a small car, I'll cheerfully kill you."

Competent masculine hands moved over her

shoulder blades and down her spine, massaging and kneading the tight muscles. His mouth made gentle contact with her mouth, rubbing and lifting and nibbling the berry-glossed softness. But Quintin found his efforts totally one-sided. "Are you trying to tell me that my inherent charm is failing to alleviate your pain and suffering?"

"Yes." Stevie's forehead fell against his shoulder. "I'm too pooped to pucker." She smiled at the rumble of laughter that reverberated in his chest.

"Go soak in a hot tub," came his soft directive. "I'll recork the wine for another time and lock the door on my way out."

She pressed a kiss into the hollow of his throat. "Quintin Ward, you are a wonderfully understanding man."

He lifted her chin, his eyes darkening under tempered emotions. "That's because you, Stephanie Brandt, are such a rare find."

6

~~~~~~~~~~~~~~~~~~

Quintin decided to prolong the moment. He lagged farther and farther behind Stevie and the white-jacketed waiter who was leading them to a private corner booth. Once her red fox coat had been checked, he was able to savor the soft architecture of sapphire-blue silk that flowed and defined Stevie's womanly contours.

Morning, noon and especially at night Quintin found his imagination captured by her. Just thinking about Stevie enlivened an otherwise dull day. He discovered how easy it was for his mind to recall visual souvenirs of their evenings together.

His ears rang with the echo of her smoky voice and low, vibrant laugh; his eyes imagined the rich molten fire that was her hair; his nose remembered the potent scent that seared his senses. Quintin's tongue suddenly circled dry lips, but he found it was Stevie he tasted.

Stephanie Brandt reminded him of a diamond: Her many facets attracted and tantalized. Quintin quickly realized that he wanted full possession of this jewellike woman. In so short a time she had succeeded in filling a void in his life that he had thought would always remain empty. He had been involved with a few women over the years and they had been wonderful, but he just couldn't love them. And now . . .

"What a charming place!" Stevie smiled at Quintin as she slid across the red leather banquette seat. Her gaze toured the Ming Terrace. The restaurant's black grass-cloth walls were decorated with delicate silk fabric paintings, brass objets d'art and rice-paper fans. Tables were strategically arranged for cozy tête-à-têtes, and booths like theirs were cloaked in red-curtained intimacy.

The atmosphere was mysterious, secretive and decidedly erotic. Stevie felt an unfamiliar warmth steal over her face and quickly shielded her blushing features behind the monstrous menu.

Dithering. Her subconscious fairly screamed the accusation. *If you were here with a client, you'd be grumbling at the lack of adequate lighting and the overdone decor. But you've been a nervous, indecisive creature since you rolled out of bed.*

Column A merged with Column B and blurred into Column C. Stevie furiously tried to blink more than the menu into focus. She was president of a company, for heaven's sake, a brisk, bright, down-to-earth overachiever. She had never dithered over anything or anyone in her thirty years—not even Paul, the man she was once engaged to marry.

Stevie took a quick peek around the menu and breathed a sigh of relief upon noting that her companion was diligently perusing three pages of delectable Chinese entrees. Quintin Ward. He was the man causing all the silliness.

Wasn't she going home tonight to a bed covered by seventy-five percent of her closet? That morning she had tried on every suit, skirt and blouse combination and every dress she owned just to find something that was just . . . just so.

Her fingers fluffed out the full sleeves that were anchored at her elbows with wide buttoned cuffs before moving to straighten the braided strands of silver and lapis chains that highlighted the dress's bateau neckline.

She frowned at her fingernails, still not liking the bisque-colored polish. Of course, she'd only painted them six different times last night. Her cuticles would never be the same!

Crossing her long legs, Stevie fleetingly wondered what Quintin thought about her final choices. She had drifted out of her house on a heavier cloud of Shalimar than usual because he had mentioned that he liked her perfume. And her dress—wasn't blue supposed to be a man's favorite color? Maybe her eyeshadow was too soft and her lipstick too bright. Were the matching earrings too much with the necklace?

Stevie choked down a semihysterical laugh. Clothes, makeup, jewelry, perfume—these items had never concerned her to such a degree before. She had always been self-conscious about her height and her figure, which despite regular exercise tended to be more ample than the fashion pages dictated.

And yet, since knowing Quintin, she felt more confident of her femininity, more comfortable with her body and more relaxed with herself. How different a person she had become. Her tawny brows puckered in thought. But had she really changed?

Her level of competence at the office was not affected. As a matter of fact, her energy seemed at an all-time high. She felt revitalized and stimulated; decisions came more easily and quickly. She was still saying yes and no; she was still forceful and assertive.

In thinking about her appearance, Stevie realized that she had selected that particular dress because that shade of blue was her favorite color and the style suited her. Shalimar had been her perfume for over ten years, and her jewelry wasn't new. Manicured or not, her hands still operated the self-service gas pump!

Still, Stevie acknowledged that a metamorphosis had occurred in those intangible areas that made up her feminine fiber. An elusive magic revived feelings that she had thought dead. And the sorcerer who made the magic was Quintin Ward.

The round-faced waiter cleared his throat three times before either of them noticed. "Stevie?" Quintin's knee nudged hers beneath the table. "Have you decided?"

She smiled at both men. "What is your chef's specialty?" Stevie inquired, and sat blinking in bewilderment as a singsong list was issued.

"We'll have the luncheon for two." Quintin took command and plucked the menu out of her hand to give to the waiter. "Tea now, please." His dark head bowed the diminutive man away.

"What is it you've ordered?" she inquired. Her voice was whispered, but the closed curtain that cocooned their booth seemed to demand low tones.

"I haven't the vaguest idea," came his dry response.

She made an elaborate display of shaking out the white linen napkin. "I trust you."

"Do you?"

Hazel eyes never faltered in their direct gaze. "Yes."

His hand sought hers; the tips of his fingers delineated each slender, polished digit. "Is your work schedule any easier this week?"

"No." Auburn tresses swished against her neck. "But so far this weekend is clear. Next Saturday I fly to Los Angeles for the American Music Award ceremonies."

"Do you mind all the traveling?" His thumb continued to stroke her wrist. Beneath the table his knee once again sought contact with hers. Quintin found himself cursing the navy suit material that imprisoned his legs when he so craved the sensual smoothness only her sleek limbs could offer.

Stevie wondered if he could feel how rapidly her pulse was beating. The prickliest sensations were dancing up her arm, swirling warmly around her breasts and snaking ever so hotly even lower. "I'm like a little kid in an airplane," she confessed, her voice an octave below normal. "I watch the movies, listen to the stereo, trade places if needed for a window seat—and I even like the food," she said, laughing. "But Nashville is hosting more award shows, so sometimes I only travel as far as the 'Opry.'"

"Tell me more about what you do." Quintin's request was more like a demand. Educating himself on every facet of her life was essential for his own well-being.

Her expression registered both surprise and pleasure. "Well, the music industry could be compared to the stock market," Stevie said, "sometimes bullish, sometimes bearish. Right now it's hurting financially. Record companies are axing artists and employees by the dozen, and the pirating problem has plundered sales.

"Consumers have tightened their purse strings, and impulse buying is less frequent. Record and tape sales were down, while video game sales gave the industry a boost. I've been aggressively exploiting music video—focusing my clients on vidisk, screen clips and MTV, the twenty-four-hour music cable channel."

Stevie warmed to her subject with natural enthusiasm. "It's quite a challenge, Quint, to develop an artist and work on his performance image. We book TV appearances, set up road tours, create promotional videocassettes and make sure the artist knows what to say and when to say it."

Quintin's eyes held even more respect. "You certainly have more than the usual business responsibilities. How do you manage?"

"In the beginning I felt totally disoriented and terrified," came her ready admission. "When my father retired and I took over, the obstacles—both personal and professional—kept mounting. But I was determined not to give up, so I kept swinging." Her lips curved in an easy smile. "Slowly the outlook began to improve. Clients and employees began to trust my judgment and decisions. Those who couldn't were replaced by those who could. And now Brandt Associates is sailing on calm waters and—"

"What's the matter?" Quintin asked. "Why did you stop?"

Her flustered tone echoed her agitated demeanor. "Because I'm supposed to be encouraging you to talk about yourself and your career, not vice versa."

He blinked in confusion, then laughed. "Is this carved in stone somewhere?"

She deliberated for a long moment and nodded.

"Yes, I think it is. At least that's what my mother told me," Stevie added demurely.

"Don't believe it," Quintin admonished, not trying to hide his amusement. "I find you more than interesting." His voice deepened. "I find you fascinating."

The tea arrived. As Stevie poured the pungent liquid into handleless cups, she thought about Quintin's compliment. She was becoming more and more self-conscious, and when she spilled some of the steaming brew on the pristine white cloth, that feeling escalated. "I make a terrible geisha," she babbled, using her napkin to daub at the stain. "I also can't dance or play the lute and I'm banned from singing in three states."

"But a geisha's main art is to please a man," he countered, his long fingers curling around the fragile china cup.

"How very chauvinistic, Mr. Ward," came her silken drawl. "Don't you think a man should learn to please a woman?"

Quintin's black pupils eclipsed their brown irises. "I think the perfect solution is for each to please the other and, in doing so, discover even greater pleasures for themselves."

"Confucius couldn't have said it better," Stevie said, smiling.

"Wisdom comes with age, and I'm just now discovering who gives me pleasure."

Her lashes fluttered like black lace wings. "And who does?"

"Stephanie Brandt."

"Why?"

"Because you know yourself. You listen to the input of others but ultimately make your own decisions. You don't fulfill a role, you create it. I feel as if I've come home whenever I'm with you, and . . ." Quintin paused for a moment, waiting to gauge her reaction. ". . . I love the idea of waking up next to you."

The sincerity of his declaration robbed her of coherent thought. He was saying all the words she had been praying to hear, and still she felt the need to proceed with teasing caution. "You're just as precocious as your son." The moment Stevie mentioned Rob, she saw Quintin undergo a change. Her hand quickly captured his. "I'm sorry. I meant to be coy, not cruel. I—"

"No, you're right." With his free hand he loosened the knot on his navy-and-pewter-striped tie. "We can't go forward until this problem with Rob is solved. So far my plan has proved to be less than brilliant."

The waiter made a second appearance, deftly bearing a massive round tray filled with covered dishes of assorted sizes. He introduced each recipe with a flourish, shrugging in bewilderment at his customers' lack of enthusiasm.

"You proved too appetizing a candy. Instead of Rob's getting sick of you, he's craving more," Quintin remarked. He looked up from spooning crisp vegetables and pork over white rice. "I can understand his cravings. You hold a fatal attraction for anyone named Ward."

Shrimp and noodles got stuck in her throat. "I . . . I didn't do it intentionally." Stevie jumped to her own defense. "I did my best to show him how foolish our dates were."

"I know that." He ignored the Occidental cutlery in favor of ornate chopsticks. "But let's be honest: You are in an industry that sells its products and makes the bulk of its profits from teen-agers. You probably don't even realize how well you fit in."

"How well I fit in!" she echoed. "I felt like the proverbial stranger in a strange land, Quintin. I didn't speak or understand their language; I was wearing the wrong clothes; their customs were totally foreign. I was darn uncomfortable," she grumbled. "I couldn't wait to get home and in my own environment. I—" Stevie stopped; a brilliant spark invaded her weary spirit. "Quint, how comfortable would Robbie be in my world?"

He waved his chopsticks in confusion.

"My secretary has stockpiles of engraved invitations to boring little social gatherings where everyone professes to love everyone else, gossip is traded with barracuda smiles and the only food served is bait on a Ritz." Her smile grew smug. "We're talking black tie every night. How long would it take for Robbie to balk at another evening of tight collars, real shoes and no health food? He won't understand the language or the customs, and while some of the people are *stars*, they have little

111

use for the 'star-struck.'" Stevie leaned back against the red leather upholstery. "I bet your son gets very bored, very fast. What do you think?"

"I think you're brilliant." Quintin lifted his teacup in salute. "When can you start?"

"Tonight. When Rob comes to work, I'll hit him with an invitation before he can issue one of his own."

"Don't forget about school tomorrow," he admonished, once again assuming his parental duties. "I don't want his grades to suffer. I think he mentioned a big exam coming up next week."

"You can't have your cake and eat it too," she countered quickly. "Let's deal this hand fast and furious and bombard Bobby with an event a night. He can cram for the exam on the weekend."

"You're right. If I issue a curfew or complain about his studies, Rob'll get belligerent again. We're getting along much better."

Stevie exhaled a satisfied breath. "This will work. I'm sure of it." With shared smiles they renewed their interest in the tempting Cantonese and spicy Szechwan banquet.

Quintin looked at his watch and grimaced. "We've been here two and a half hours. Your secretary's going to shoot me." He gave a cursory inspection to the check, mentally added on a tip and tossed the necessary bills on the table. "I've got a three-thirty appointment with three doctors who are interested in having a clinic built." He guided her toward the cloakroom.

"Sounds promising." Stevie slid her arms into the silk-lined sleeves of her red fox coat, which he was holding.

"Despite a general decline in construction, last year was very good for me," Quintin reported, dropping a bill into the cloakroom's tip tray and tossing his camel topcoat over his arm. "This year is looking even better. Why don't you stay inside while I bring around the car."

Her hand curved around his wrist. "I think I'd better take a cab. Rob will be reporting for work anytime, and if he sees your BMW . . ."

"Damn. I don't like all this subterfuge." Quintin gave a rough push to the restaurant's glass door. "I feel like a sneak, as if we're doing something illicit." He motioned for a nearby on-duty cab. "Of course, there is something very sexy about clandestine encounters." His dark brows lifted suggestively.

Quintin's hand sank into the rich fullness of Stevie's hair, pulling her head the scant few inches needed to make contact with her lips. The kiss was hard and quick but nonetheless exciting, and when it was over, Stevie had difficulty recovering her breath and her poise to tell the cabbie where to go.

"I really thought this was going to work, Gloria." Stevie sighed for the third time and stared forlornly into the fragrant orange and spice tea that shimmered in the white china cup. "Monday I dragged Bobby to the art museum's cubist exhibit and we sat in uncomfortable, unpadded chairs for three hours, listening to a lecture that was followed by a flute concert. Tuesday was a real opera at the 'Opry.' Wednesday, the ballet at the Performing Arts Center, and tonight—" She paused and looked at her secretary. "Where is it we're going tonight?"

Gloria leafed through her steno pad. "Back to the 'Opry' to hear the gospel groups practice for the Dove Award ceremonies, and a party at the Carstairs."

"The kid should be exhausted. I know I am." Stevie sagged into the bolstered comfort of the leather executive chair. "He should gag when he looks at his tux; I know it takes me an hour to get up enough courage to even look through my closet and find something formal to wear. That damn kid should be bored!"

"The roses are still coming," Gloria reminded her boss. "What does Papa Ward say?"

"We talk on the phone every night until one of us falls asleep. Quint says Bobby still whistles all the way up the stairs after I drop him home."

"Some women have it and some women don't!"

Stevie made an ugly face. "I want to 'it' the father, not the son."

"Like that, huh?"

"Like that," Stevie concurred. "I miss seeing Quintin. Between my schedule and the late nights, all I get to do is hear his voice. Cuddling the telephone is not the same." She gulped a mouthful of lukewarm tea. "Do you have any suggestions on how to deal with Bobby?"

"Are you kidding? I can't figure out my own teen-agers, let alone somebody else's." Her pencil point tapped the notepad. "Back to work, sweetie; the correspondence is piling up and so are the demo tapes. I spread a few around to lighten your In basket; you can review the reports."

"How many people are we down?"

"Between the flu and vacations, about fifteen, and if you keep up this insane schedule," Gloria warned, "you'll be dictating from a sanatorium."

"Right now that sounds mighty tempting!"

Stevie turned off the shower spray, slid open the etched glass doors and listened. "That's the doorbell!" Dripping arms were jerked into terrycloth sleeves while the rest of the thick robe was bundled and belted around her shivering body. The luminous dial on her digital alarm showed six A.M. as Stevie sprinted out of the bedroom.

"Quintin!" She pulled him inside and stared at the rugged face that looked drawn and pinched, gray flesh bagged under his eyes. "What is it? You look awful."

"I haven't slept. I prowled around the house all night; my poor housekeeper thought we had a burglar."

Compassionate eyes silently watched Quintin's private torment. "Do you want some coffee?" After she made the offer, Stevie wondered if, in his agitated condition, he could handle the added stimulation of caffeine.

"Yes. No." His hand made a series of confused movements.

She took a deep breath, grabbed his wrist and led him into the living room. "Tell me what's the matter."

"Rob."

"Oh, God," her hand went to her throat, "he didn't . . . didn't run away or—"

"No." His fingers ravaged his dark hair. "No. He's still asleep." Quintin leaned back, resting his exhausted body in the lush confines of the sofa. "Last night, after you dropped him home, Rob spent an hour telling me that the past week has been the highlight of his life. How wonderful all your friends were to him; what a great time he had being with you day and night; that you are the sweetest, sincerest, kindest, most caring woman he'd ever met."

"Oh, no!"

"Oh, yes!" His fist pummeled his thigh. "That damn kid outsmarts us at every turn."

Stevie's shoulders slumped; her dejected expression matched his. "Now what? Frankly, Quintin, I can't think of anything else to do." Her fingers stroked his still-tight fist. "I'd offer to extend my stay in California next week and hope time and distance would solve the problem, but I just don't have the luxury of that option right now."

"I know." His hand made a weary pass over his eyes, his chest heaving under stress. "I've been trying to think of something that would end this and end it fast." Quintin avoided looking at her, concentrating instead on the wooden buttons and rope toggles that decorated his sheepskin jacket. "I . . . I think we should try a scare tactic."

"What kind of scare tactic?" Each word was expelled with cool deliberation.

"I think you should take him into the more"—Quintin swallowed—"lurid music world."

"What!" Her hand grabbed his jaw, jerking his face toward her. "Are you crazy! I told you before I'm not into the drug scene or the wild parties or—"

"But you know who is."

"Well, yes, but—"

"And you know where they are?"

"Yes, but—"

"And you could get invited and you could bring Rob and you could shock the hell out of him."

"It would shock me too!" came her vehement protest. "Quintin, this is insane." Stevie stood up, her back forming a barrier that was just as emphatic as her words. "I will not do it."

He moved behind her; his hands curved around her upper arms. "Listen to me. I have really thought this through. I didn't just dream it up; I remembered that TV show a few years back, *Scared Straight*. They brought teen-agers into prisons and let the convicts tell and show them how things really were and what could happen to them."

"And you think this brilliant scheme is going to mirror that?" Her response was sarcastic.

"It's a viable idea." Quintin's voice rose defensively. "That show worked. They still air the program in high schools. If you take Rob out of his normal element and show him you're no Pollyanna, it will destroy this fantasy image he has of you."

Quintin took a deep breath and pressed home his final point. "I want to get this monkey off my back. I want to get my son focused on all the right things a seventeen-year-old boy should be interested in. And then I can focus on all the things a thirty-nine-year-old man should be interested in."

He pulled Stevie around, his fingers combing back the wet auburn curls. "Do you know how long this week was for me? How totally inadequate just talking to you is when I so desperately need to see you, touch you, taste you." His mouth swooped down to claim its prey. Her lips felt just as he had remembered: soft, warm, compelling.

His hands traveled over her shoulders and down her back, pressing into the base of her spine to meld her body against his. "I need to hold you like this every day, every night. Just touching you brings me life." Quintin husked the admission into the soap-scented curve of her neck. "Without you I feel so damn empty, so unfillable."

Stevie's hand moved inside the jacket; her fingertips encountered his rapidly beating heart. "It's been terrible for me too," came her whispered confession. "You're all that I think about."

He pounced on her words. "Please, Stevie." He stared bleakly at her. "Do this and we can be together. Forever."

"All . . . all right, Quintin." She swallowed her own aversion. "I'll set something up for tonight."

7

~~~~~~~~~~~~~

Quintin's leather-booted foot pushed open the left side of the double front doors. He backed into the brightly lit entry foyer juggling two briefcases, a cylinder containing blueprints and the evening paper. Everything but the *Banner* clattered to the marble floor. He viewed the fallen chaos with discouraged eyes; how well it represented the last twenty-four hours.

The steady tempo of a basketball bouncing against wooden steps heralded Rob's arrival long before his cheery "Hi, Dad" was issued. "Mrs. Crawford's holding what's left of a great pot roast for you if you haven't had dinner." One glance at the cluttered floor and his father's face effectively curtailed any further dribbling. "Rough day, huh?" Rob offered a smile. "I want to ask you . . ."

A wave of tenderness washed over Quintin. He found he had to blink hard. This was his flesh and blood. A son who would make any father proud.

He found it easy to conjure up the past. He recalled powdering and diapering Rob's bottom, worrying about which ointment would ease the discomfort of a rash that never seemed to go away. He remembered the little airplane games he would play to try to get his baby son to eat new foods, and the countless baskets of clothes he had laundered when assorted strained fruits and vegetables were spittingly rejected.

Quintin's thumb ached under a phantom bite from a nine-month-old baby who cried and drooled into teething. He could hear Rob's delighted laughter at being taken to the park and could see all the mud puddles that had been trampled through over the years.

There were some awful moments too: Robbie falling from his first two-wheeler and bloodying both knees; the black eye from his first fistfight and the five stitches that were needed when he had been hit in the head with a baseball bat. Quintin's most vivid recollection was the trip to the emergency room when Rob was a "terrible two" and had managed to swallow acorns that had dropped into his playpen. He had been scared to death that his son would die.

Scared to death. Quintin's stomach twisted into another knot; nausea burned in his throat. That's what was in store for his baby boy tonight. All day he had wondered about the validity of his "scared straight" idea. Maybe Stevie had been right: Perhaps his latest stroke of brilliant parental psychology was stupid. Maybe he would—

"Earth to Dad, earth to Dad!" Robbie waved a hand in front of his father's rather glazed countenance. "Hey, Dad, did you hear me? Is it all right if I spend this weekend over at Jack's? He checked it out with his folks. We're going to study for the SATs and—"

Quintin shook his head. "Wait a minute." A large hand clamped on Rob's shoulder. "Did you ask to spend *this* weekend at Jack's?" At the affirmative he tried to sound casual. "I . . . I thought for sure you and Stevie would be out on the town again tonight."

Rob gave a careless shrug. "We did have plans. Something really special, Stevie said. But she called half an hour ago and said tonight was off." He gestured toward the gym bag on the credenza. "I'm packed and set to go. Jack's got a new neighbor. Some kid named Tommie from Colorado with a 3-D camera. The pictures are supposed to be really something. Can I go?"

"Sure. Sure," came Quintin's absentminded response. He reached into the pocket of his brown tweed suit pants. "Here"—he handed his son a ten-dollar bill—"why don't you treat for pizza tomorrow."

"Hey, thanks!" He bounced the basketball toward the door. "I won't be home until seven on Sunday. We're going to watch the Super Bowl play-offs. Tommie's got one of those big-screen TV projection systems."

Quintin quelled his anger until the front door closed. His long legs ate up the distance to the study; he grabbed the receiver and punched Stevie's number into the phone. "How could you do this without checking with me," he muttered, listening to her phone ring. "Talk about nerve!" His fingers drummed impatiently against the desk.

Her voice answered, dulcet and lyrical, but it was only a recorded message. "Stevie? Stevie, can you hear me?" Quintin hoped the machine was on audition. "Stevie! I'm going to call you right back and I want some answers." He tried again. This time the line was busy.

He pressed the button for the operator. After checking, she announced in an impersonal monotone: "There is no talking on the line. The receiver is either off the hook or the phone is out of order. Shall I report it for you, sir?"

"No. I'll see to it myself."

Stevie returned to her fetal position in the white rocking chair, finding the comfortable indentation she had made in the peach satin cushion still warm. She had taken the kitchen phone off the hook; the whining signal of warning wasn't able to penetrate the quiet haven of her bedroom.

Rocking was so soothing. The constant gentle seesaw motion reminded her of the ocean and the lacy ruffled tide that edged the shore. Eyes closed,

Stevie steadily rocked and rocked, hoping to attain some inner tranquility.

While her life had been drawn in black and white, over the years Stevie had acknowledged that there were many shades of gray to contend with. She had her own code of ethics, her own virtues and honor.

What Quintin wanted her to do was wrong. She had tried to justify it all day and had failed.

So she had canceled Rob's excursion into the shocking nether regions of the music industry. Maybe she should have called Quintin, discussed her feelings with him. But he had been so dogmatic, so positive that that was the only way to go. Stevie discovered she just couldn't agree.

When the door chimes shattered her solitude, Stevie rocked harder. When fists pounded against the front door and a minute later pummeled the rear, she plugged her fingers into her ears and continued the to-and-fro movement that provided a modicum of comfort.

Quintin had seen it done many times by TV detectives, and didn't American Express say never leave home without one? So why, he grumbled, did TV shows make breaking and entering look so easy?

He wiggled the green plastic between the lock and the frame and carefully pushed sideways. He heard a snap, smiled in delight, then swore. He was now the proud owner of two halves of an unusable charge card and still faced a locked door.

He leveled a frustrated kick at the brick planter and then suddenly remembered Stevie's extra key. Was it always hidden there or . . . his searching hand discovered the cool metal shielded by masking tape.

"Stevie!"

Her roared name caused her to wince and curl tighter into the Boston rocker. Her bedroom door was closed, the house dark. Stevie decided to play possum and maybe Quintin would go away.

"I knew you were here."

Hazel eyes widened slightly as the hallway light cast his tall, muscular figure in harsh silhouette. Feet apart, hands on hips, he stood before her. "You're rather presumptuous," she returned. "Since both the phone and bell went unanswered, one would assume you'd get the general message." Her inflection was totally devoid of any of the emotions that raged within.

"I'm presumptuous?" came his sarcastic rebuttal. "You're the one who had the effrontery to overrule my parental judgment."

Stevie's bare feet thudded against the ivory carpet; she pushed herself free of the rocker. "You aren't using judgment, parental or otherwise," she railed, her hands curling into impotent fists at her sides. "Sometimes, Quintin, you show absolutely no sign of intelligence at all."

He bristled under the insult. "Now, wait just one minute—"

"No, you wait." Her forefinger stabbed rudely into his chest. "I've spent the last two weeks getting to know your son. Really know him. Bobby's gentle and sensitive and kind and caring. And what you wanted me to do tonight would have hurt and confused him. Damn it, Quintin, I love your son."

"You . . . you what?" Her words dealt him a forceful blow. He staggered backward; the edge of the bed caught the back of his knees; he sat down hard on the peach satin bedspread. "What do you mean you love my son? That's . . . you . . . I . . ." Quintin discovered that his brain had lost its connection with his vocal cords.

Stevie's tone was as soft as the hands that caressed his face. "Why can't I love your son?" Her fingertips gently pressed along his proud cheekbones, then meandered down to explore his strong, stubborn jaw. "Rob is you. His eyes are your eyes. His face is your face." Her fingernail traced his firm lips. "His mouth is your mouth."

She took a deep breath, hazel eyes glittering like polished stones in the dusky light. "I could never hurt Rob because I could never hurt you. I love your son because he is you." Her hands cupped his face. "And I love you so very much."

Quintin's arms wrapped her in a sinewy prison, pressing her trembling body tightly against his. "Stevie. Oh, Stevie. Stevie." He rained joyful kisses over her forehead, nose and chin. "Do you know how many times I've dreamed of hearing you say that?" His voice was low and husky. "Terrified that you never would."

He succumbed to the intoxicating temptation of her lips. His mouth was at first bruising in its possession, anxious to secure ownership of the valuable treasure that was this woman's love. Suddenly his kiss changed, his lips enjoying the soft fullness of hers, his wanton tongue seeking to explore the honeyed recesses beyond.

Stevie felt free to match his ardor. Her fingernails fluttered in an erotic dance against his nape. Her tongue reacted in sensual abandon to its mate and made teasing forays of its own.

"Do you know how much I love you?" he rasped, his lips blazing a warm trail down the center of her throat.

Her hands cupped his face, her eyes more eloquent than words. "Show me." Stevie whispered the provocative challenge against his mouth. "I love the idea of waking up in your arms."

A pleasurable groan escaped Quintin as his lips slanted hungrily over hers, his tongue thrusting a primitive message of acceptance. Masculine hands sought to conquer every inch of silk-covered skin, roaming over her shoulders and back and moving down her supple spine.

"Oh . . ." A low moan came from deep in her throat, expressing her own urgency. Her body felt on fire, her skin burning from Quintin's heated touch.

Virile fingers quickly dispensed with the five buttons that locked Stevie behind a wall of liquid midnight; the navy nightshirt drifted into a silken pool around her feet. "You are so beautiful." Quintin's voice trembled with raw emotion.

He buried his face in the fragrant opulence of her

hair; her perfume enveloped his senses, heightening them like a narcotic. He swayed slightly, his arms tightening their hold around her as they tumbled onto the bed.

Quintin released her for only the time it took to litter the plush carpet with a variety of masculine clothes. Roughly he pulled her into his arms. "You feel so good against me."

Stevie literally purred, finding herself very responsive to the hands that lavished praise on her breasts. She anxiously surveyed the rugged landscape of his physique. Her fingers frolicked amid the dark hair that curled thickly on his sinewy chest and unhesitantly followed the furry trail lower.

His mouth pressed hot, eager kisses across her breasts. His tongue bathed her in a warm dampness, teasing and arousing the shy nipples so that he could suckle the taut peaks. His palm moved across her stomach, fingers seeking the sensitive skin of her inner thigh.

Her legs parted willingly, allowing her to enjoy the sensuous intrusion of his probing finger. She moaned in delicious abandon as exquisite little currents jolted her body.

Stevie sought to bring equal pleasure to Quintin, boldly moving her hand lower; tender fingers circled the throbbing maleness that continued to blossom under gentle caresses. His answering moans of delight only succeeded in intensifying her own passions.

Quintin loomed over her; his hands slid beneath her buttocks, lifting her to receive him. Stevie caught her breath, loving that a part of him was now within her. Two individuals briefly became one in a joyful union that was based on shared love and respect.

For a while they luxuriated in private pleasures that brought their bodies closer and closer to the precipice of ecstasy. Quintin seemed to know instinctively the rhythm that would bring Stevie the most pleasure. His lovemaking was rich and vital, and she eagerly surrendered to it.

She pulled his head down, needing to feel the security of his firm lips. Her body rippled with inner explosions. Her fingernails sank into Quintin's shoulders as she was submerged under waves of rapture.

Quintin cried out, himself out of control, his rugged frame crumbling; his love offering poured deep within her. "God, I love you." His words were barely audible under his own inner trembling.

Each was a willing captive of the other and both at peace in the culmination of their love. Stevie pressed a thankful kiss against Quintin's shoulder, her tongue savoring his salty flesh. "I love you, Quintin Ward." She felt warm, safe, secure and, for the first time, complete.

His hand smoothed her silken hair, his legs wrapping hers in intimacy. "I love you more."

Stevie cuddled closer, her breasts snug against his torso, her arms wrapped around him. "When did it happen? When did you know?"

"Somewhere between the pizza and the chow mein"—his hand traveled the sensuous waist to hip curve to settle on her buttock—"just around the bubble gum." The teasing lightness in his voice turned serious. "To tell you the truth, it was the strangest thing. I just wanted to be with you all the time, see you every day. And after I did, I felt wonderful. The sky looked bluer, the clouds fluffier and whiter; everything and everyone looked beautiful. Does that make any sense?"

"Yes." Her lips moved against his neck. "I found myself thinking about you all the time," Stevie admitted, "and that had never happened with anyone before. Despite all your growling, you are a sensitive, passionate man." She lifted her head; the lambent sheen in her eyes glowed in the dusky light. "I think I love your sensitivity more than anything else. A man that can feel and express his emotions is a man to be cherished."

"No, love"—Quintin hugged her tight—"you're to be cherished and not just for one night. Stevie, I'm not playing a game," he warned. "I'll always be here for you, and I have to know you'll always be there for me."

She placed a tender kiss on the corner of his mouth. "Forever," Stevie promised. "I can't think what it was like before you. I don't want a life without you." She took a deep breath and expressed the one fault in their perfect world. "About Robbie . . ."

"Shhh." His fingers stilled her lips. "Rob's staying with his friend Jack till Sunday. I'll go home tomorrow, pack a few things and leave your number with my housekeeper in case of an emergency." Quintin moved her head back into the curve of his neck. "This weekend is for us. You and me. No one else."

His hand snagged the hem of the satin comforter, and with a quick tug he enveloped them in downy luxury. Basking in the afterglow of loving, they presently succumbed to sleep.

The aroma of freshly brewed coffee stirred Stevie from sensual lethargy. Eyes closed, she stretched like a satisfied kitten, content and serene. Her cheek snuggled against the plump pillow, her nose inhaling Quintin's clean, masculine scent from the apricot percale.

Reaching for him, Stevie found the bed empty. "Quintin!" She sat up, blinking the room into focus. "Quintin?" Her voice revealed her anxiety.

"Stay right there," he caroled. "Don't move a muscle or you'll spoil my surprise."

Laughing at her initial panic, she propped the pillows behind her back and pulled the peach-toned sheets into a modest cover that shielded her nude form. "What are you up to?"

The bedroom door was kicked open. "Breakfast in bed." Quintin grinned, displaying a white wicker bed tray, its contents hidden beneath a large white linen napkin. "While you were snoring away"—his eyebrows jiggled in amusement—"I was slaving over a hot oven to bring you the ultimate indulgence."

She looked curiously at the cranberry velour robe that wrapped his virile length. "You've already been home?"

Quintin placed the tray across her legs and sat on the edge of the bed. "I wanted to get that out of the way so our time wouldn't be interrupted." His dark eyes feasted on her sleepy beauty.

His hands splayed through the vibrant russet waves, fingers gently straightening the tumbled curls. His lips bestowed fourteen quick butter-soft kisses, one on each of the freckles spangled across her nose. "I hated to fall asleep last night," Quintin whispered, his beard-roughened cheek nuzzling the smooth curve of her jaw. "I wanted to hold you, touch you, kiss you. I was so afraid I was dreaming."

"You weren't dreaming, my darling, you weren't dreaming." Stevie's arms circled his neck, her lips warm and passionate as they enjoyed a glorious reunion with his mouth. "Was I dreaming this morning or did we . . ."

His forefinger patted the tip of her straight nose. "I needed something to get me motivated or you would have never gotten this delectable breakfast." With a flourish Quintin lifted the napkin covering. "Hot croissants, French-roast coffee and mimosas, plus a sprig of January jasmine from my garden."

Stevie lifted the yellow flower, inhaling the heady fragrance of the gelsemium. She smiled at him. "I hadn't realized you were such a gourmet."

Quintin tucked the dainty sprig behind her ear.

"To be honest, love, I raided my own kitchen. My housekeeper will find the bread box and the refrigerator a little lighter than they were last night." He moved around the bed and slid beneath the covers.

They fed each other oven-warmed croissants dripping with butter and piqued with raspberry jam. The coffee was rich and mellow but it was the mimosas, orange juice dignified with cognac and bubbled by champagne, that kept them lingering in bed until late in the afternoon.

"There, Quintin, now you know all about Stephanie Brandt, from birth to age thirty." She pressed a kiss against his chest. "Quintin? Quintin!" Coming up on one elbow, she scrutinized his sleeping face. "Well, really." Stevie sniffed and pretended annoyance. "The man asks for my life story and has the nerve to fall asleep. Was it that boring?"

"I'm not sleeping." Eyes still closed, his mouth curved into a smile. "I'm just resting my eyes. You could never be a bore. And I certainly know better than to feed you liver, brussels sprouts and turnip greens." One brown eye opened and closed in a quick wink. "See, I was listening."

Stevie's gaze wandered the lean length of him, the thin top sheet molded to his naked body. Memories of his lovemaking sent sweet sensations moving through her blood to her heart. Her fever began to rise.

The backs of her fingernails brushed a feathery massage across his torso; her fingers moved alternately up and down and in spirals, making his hair-roughened flesh tingle in response to her sensuous dallying.

"What *are* you doing?" came his husky inquiry.

"Nothing." The reply was a soft whisper.

"Hmmm. Keep on doing it."

Her tongue ran wetly around the outline of his lips, making a quick dart inside. Her lips flowed down the sensitive cord on his neck, across his chest to his left breast. Stevie could hear Quintin's heart pound in an erratic rhythm that matched her own.

She found his tough male nipple beneath the dark mat of curls, and her tongue and teeth gently bedeviled the rubbery tip. Her hands made an intimate survey of his chest, nails harassing the bottom of his ribs. Quintin's long, husky moans of pleasure only succeeded in piquing her own desire.

Stevie ventured lower, her hair spreading like a silk fan across his flat stomach. She found herself very responsive, savoring each step that led to the perfect circle of his navel, nuzzling it lightly with her lips and tongue. Her teasing fingers walked an erotic path along the top of his sinewy thighs before stroking the more sensitive flesh between.

His response was immediate, and she marveled at the power she had over this dynamic man. Her own appetite raging out of control, Stevie took his male hardness into her soft body.

Her satisfied groan echoed and merged with

Quintin's. Stevie straddled his hips and set a languid rhythm that unleashed wild, delicious sensations.

Quintin's pleasure was intense as his dark eyes observed her flushed, euphoric features. His hands stroked the sides of her body, fingers pressing into the firm flesh of her buttocks to urge tighter contact. He raised his head slightly, his lips fondling the creamy skin of her breast, tugging on the urgent rose-tipped peak.

They moved in sweet and shattering shared surrender, their passions finally exploding in a mutual release that further cemented their love.

"God, I love you." Quintin's voice was husky with emotion. "You are incredible." His kiss was soft and tender against her mouth as he hauled her trembling body into the curve of his. "I feel as if I could go out and conquer the world."

"Not me." Stevie yawned in sleepy satisfaction. Her tone was tinged with humor as she added, "These non-pizza orgies are exhausting."

Sunday morning's brunch was shattered by the urgent ring of the telephone. Stevie hesitated for a moment, her eyes locking with Quintin's before lifting the receiver. "Yes." Her auburn head nodded in silent approval for him to refill her coffee mug. "Hi, Mary. What's up? No. You tell Doug to stay home and try to shake off the flu. Really, no problem. I'll head over to the studio and supervise the taping. Bye."

Quintin secured the phone. "Trouble?" He settled on the bar stool next to hers and confiscated the last corn muffin.

"Another of my staff has been sidelined," she related, turning to squint at the stove clock. "Quint, I'm afraid my job is intruding into our intimate weekend. I have to cover a video taping in half an hour."

He leaned forward to rub his nose against hers. "No problem, love. This will give me the opportunity to see you in action."

"I hope you're up to the action," came her cryptic announcement.

The action, Quintin soon discovered as he stared in amazement through the control booth's glass viewing windows, was video's latest art form. Four of Stevie's clients were taping three- and four-minute clips for MTV, the cable channel that broadcasts rock-music video showing groups acting out their songs.

Quintin decided that the whole effect was one of making a commercial of a movie of a person clowning before a mirror. The rockers seemed self-conscious about posing, and the lip-syncing was no better than that in B-grade Japanese monster epics.

Strange things abounded in the taping. Lots of guitars were broken, firecrackers exploded, fog machines and effect lighting made an eerie nightmare sequence. The afternoon was an adventure into impoverished surrealism.

Although the video clips would have an air time

of less than five minutes, the taping lasted close to six hours. Tempers flared, both in front of and in back of the cameras; demands and insults were traded in heated anxiety. And Quintin was chagrined to learn that Stephanie Brandt could war with the best of them.

"This was not the way I had planned to spend our last day together," Stevie grumbled for the tenth time. They had no sooner returned to her house than Quintin had to leave. "I'm sorry." How ineffectual those words sounded.

He studied her forlorn expression. "I enjoyed it. Honest." His hand lifted her chin. "Damn it, but I don't want to go." Quintin looked with longing at her. "I don't think I can."

"No, darling"—her knuckles caressed his strong jaw—"Robbie will be home in twenty minutes and you've got to be there for your son. He needs you just as much as I do."

"If he ever finds out—"

She pressed her finger to his lips. "That's why you must go home and act perfectly normal. Tell him you spent all weekend working on that clinic project. I'm . . . I'm going to make sure I'm out of the office when he comes to work, and maybe in time this silly schoolboy crush will disappear."

His heavy sigh was in agreement with her comment. "When can I see you tomorrow?" came his impatient request.

Stevie smiled, lashes fluttering provocatively. "I know I'm scheduled for a dinner meeting Monday that will run very late, but are you free for lunch?"

"I'll make sure I am." His hand curved possessively around her neck, fingers sinking into the opulent auburn curls. His mouth claimed hers in a slow, lingering kiss that he knew would have to last all through the night.

8

~~~~~~~~~~~~~

"**P**apa Ward is on line one," Gloria announced over the telephone intercom, her voice raspy and brittle. Clearing her throat, she added, "He's been waiting impatiently all the while you were on that conference call."

"Thanks." Stevie punched in the line. "Good morning, darling. I missed you last night."

"Hmmm . . . not half as much as I missed you," Quintin returned huskily. "I tried calling you early this morning but all I got was your machine." His silky deep voice teased her ear. "I left a very risqué message on it."

"I'll replay it all night long. I had a New York conference call coming in at six A.M. our time. We've been having a lot of trouble with record and tape pirates and I had a nasty little go-around about doubling security with a distributor."

"Stevie, I said it before and I'll keep on saying it: You are incredible," came his humble response. "As a matter of fact, I find your business prowess very exciting."

"Quintin," she purred, "you're making me blush."

"Just the sound of your voice is doing delicious things to me. What time shall I collect you for lunch?" He sounded urgent.

She deliberated a moment, then took a deep breath. "Quintin, would you mind meeting me at the Hunt Room in Radisson Plaza? I've got an outside appointment right around the corner, and that way, if my meeting runs late, I won't have to waste time driving back here."

"Hunt Room? Very elegant, love. What time?"

"Twelve-thirty."

"Perfect." Quintin's voice deepened. "I love you, Stevie. I . . . oh, damn, my other phone is ringing and my secretary's not there. See you later, love."

Leaning back in her swivel chair, Stevie surveyed her outfit. The business suit was of traditional gray flannel, the skirt slim with a snappy side pleat, the jacket expertly tailored with a mandarin collar and silver buttons; the long-sleeved tailored blouse was a swirling mix of white and gray.

Hidden beneath the monochromatic efficiency was a cherished secret of seductive lingerie. The satiny flower-strewn chemise and matching lace-enchanted bikini made Stevie feel giddily romantic. *Romantic*—a smile curved her mauve-tinted lips— yes, that was the word, and she discovered that her femininity blossomed in the romance that invaded her previously work-oriented world.

Under Quintin's patient tutelage, her sexual confidence increased and she was more in touch with her desires and responses than she had ever dreamed possible. He made her feel so special, so valuable, so beautiful; and she felt encouraged to demonstrate the results.

Stevie had planned this luncheon scheme all the night before and had looked forward to it all morning. In between her business decisions she mentally focused on Quintin and lunch.

An article in one of the women's magazines had said that men were tremendously excited by women who took the sexual initiative. "Well," Stevie muttered, "we shall see."

While that had overtones of assertiveness, she felt that her feminine side would surface and help erase from Quintin's mind the fiasco at the taping the day before. Stevie's nose wrinkled in remembered disgust at the crude display of tempers in the recording studio.

What had happened to her patient, unflappable attitude? She had abandoned it and wallowed in rather vulgar vocal mud along with the male engineers and artists. True, there had been the need of getting her point across and quickly moving the project to completion, but her unladylike behavior was not something she was proud of, and Stevie was extremely conscious of the fact that Quintin had heard and seen her at her worst.

She was determined to erase those bad impressions and present a much softer and more womanly side of herself to Quintin. Rubbing her hands in giddy anticipation, she redirected her attention to the file marked For Your Signature. Twenty minutes later, her fingers flexing from writer's cramp, Stevie placed the empty folder on Gloria's desk. "All done and in my Out basket. I even licked all the envelopes." Her amiable grin faded. "Say, are you all right? You look . . . flushed."

Gloria cleared her throat. "It's this red dress." She coughed and cleared her throat again. "I'm fine."

"You're not fine." Stevie felt the older woman's forehead. "You've got a fever." She reached over and flicked off the electric typewriter. "Go home."

"I can't." The typewriter was flipped back on. "Do you see this steno book? It's filled with letters that need transcribing; all those rejected tapes need to be packed up and sent with the appropriate 'Thanks but no thanks' notes, and—" She interrupted her own protest with a spasm of coughing.

Stevie walked around and yanked the typewriter's plug out of the wall. "Call that temporary secretarial service we've used a couple of times and see if you can get someone in here who knows their eight-tracks from their cassettes. Then go home, have some chicken soup and aspirins and be back here next Monday."

"I can't be gone a whole week," Gloria protested. "You're too busy and—"

"Either take the week off or I'll fire you," Stevie returned with an easy smile. "Listen, lady, you are too important around here. I need you healthy to man the helm; remember, I head for LA Saturday morning."

"If you put it that way . . ." Gloria's blue eyes blinked a watery thank-you behind her bifocals. Her fingers swiftly hunted through the Rolodex for the temporary's number. "Have you made any changes in your schedule?"

"Lunch might run a tad long," came Stevie's insouciant comment.

"Like that, huh."

"Hmmmm."

"Good afternoon, sir."

Quintin nodded to the maître d' who presided over the Hunt Room. "I'm to meet Miss Stephanie Brandt for lunch."

"Ah, yes. Mr. Ward, this is for you."

Brown eyes bleakly contemplated the sealed white envelope. Quintin retired behind a potted palm, dreading to read that lunch had been canceled. *Well,* he mentally chastised his slowly deflating ego, *one of the things you love most about her is her business savvy and dedication to her career and clients.*

He didn't consider Stevie's work a rival. He wanted their life together to be a true fifty-fifty proposition and knew that equality and flexibility would be of utmost importance. So right now, while his commitments were light and hers were heavy, Quintin acknowledged that he'd be the one making allowances.

He ripped the seal on the ivory watermark bond. The note inside bore only three notations: Room 333—S. Perplexed, Quintin followed the instructions. He walked out of the restaurant, through the lobby of the Radisson Plaza and into an elevator that whisked him to the third floor.

Quintin gave a gentle rap on the hotel room door, hoping he wasn't interrupting crucial client negotiations. The door opened; familiar hazel eyes examined him and a hand snaked out to pull him inside. "What—"

"Hi!" Stevie wrapped her arms around Quintin's neck, her scantily covered curves pressing against his rugged frame.

A blunt forefinger lifted her chin. "And here I thought I was being stood up for a business meeting." His eyes radiated delight. "But I can see you're hardly dressed for business." Quintin's hand flowed over the posy-strewn satin, coming to rest under the chemise's waist-high slit.

"I am dressed for a meeting," she teased as her fingernails drew erotic squiggles amid the dark waves that hugged the back of his head. Her glittering eyes looked deeply into his, her voice low and whispery. "Last night, while I was wallowing in the bathtub, my thoughts centered totally on you."

Her lashes fluttered provocatively. "I realized that I had never seen you covered with bubbles. So I decided to create this romantic rendezvous."

Stevie took Quintin's hand and led him past the outer living-room area, into and through a mammoth bedroom, to the bathroom. "We like to use this suite to put up our out-of-town clients because it has such a nice luxurious perk." She nodded toward a garden of thriving greenery that framed a Roman-style sunken tub. The blue marble–tiled fixture was frothy with bubbling white suds that owed their vitality to pulsating Jacuzzi jets. A nearby tray held an ice-filled dish heavy with giant sea prawns, two glasses and a split of champagne. "What do you think?"

Quintin's fingers drifted across her bare shoulders to slide the thin lingerie straps down her arms. "I think we're both overdressed." The slinky lace chemise slithered to the floor, leaving Stevie clad in the tiniest of panties.

"Speaking of overdressed . . ." came her teasing rejoinder. Efficient hands removed his Shetland tweed sport coat and gray tie. She took longer with his blue shirt, bestowing a warm kiss against his broad chest after each button was undone.

With a low groan Quintin halted Stevie's progress, pulling her into his arms. She wiggled provocatively, her full breasts harassing the curly mat of hair that covered his sinewy torso.

"Last night seemed endless without you"—his cheek rubbed against hers—"and then when I thought lunch was going to be canceled . . ." His tongue slashed apart her lips, his mouth conquering their glossy ripeness with hungry ardor.

The satisfied moan in Stevie's throat was consumed by Quintin. Their lips and tongues enjoyed a feverish, intimate duel that left them breathless and glowing with anticipation.

"I've been absolutely giddy about doing this all morning," Stevie confessed, her voice husky with desire. She fumbled with the buckle on his belt, released the hook and lowered the zipper; his gray slacks collapsed on the tile.

Shoes and socks were quickly dispatched and they stood facing each other in their briefs. Quintin stroked her body, his hands filling with her breasts before moving along the taut skin of her stomach. Her fingertips pressed along the working muscles of his back, loving the rippling strength hidden beneath the tough flesh.

As his fingers encountered and rolled down her lace panties, her thumbs hooked into the waistband of his navy briefs. Together they eliminated the last vestiges of their manmade trappings and stepped into a sudsy hedonistic environment.

"I was right." Stevie smeared creamy foam over his chest. "You look even more masculine covered in bubbles."

"And you"—he dotted each rosy nipple with lather—"look even more feminine." They moved to sit on the tub's lowest step, wallowing in the luxury of the swirling water. "This was a wonderful idea." Quintin sighed, his right leg looping over hers as they sat shoulder to shoulder.

"I'm glad you approve." Stevie reached for a shrimp, dipping the tender pink meat into a container of lemoned cocktail sauce. "I did promise you lunch."

His even white teeth bit into the chilled delicacy, his eyes widening at the potency of the horseradish-laden topping. "Whew!" Quintin's eyelids tried to disperse the tears.

Stevie quickly handed him a glass of champagne. "Too much?"

He cooled his tongue. "Perfect," came his laughing pronouncement.

She sighed and pulled the tray closer. "How was Rob last night?"

"Fine." Quintin nodded, feeding her a prawn. "He had a good weekend with Jack and some new kid named Tommie who has a 3-D camera that is 'like totally total,'" he mimicked.

Stevie took a sip of the sparkling wine. "I have a late meeting at United Artists, so I won't be seeing him today. I think that will help."

"Don't worry, love." His fingers sifted among the thick copper-gold waves that were brushed back from a barely discernible widow's peak. "Everything will get straightened out, and then you'll be in my home as my wife."

She smiled at him. "I'd love nothing better, but not at the expense of losing your son."

"What about if we—"

Her champagne glass formed a seal on his

mouth. "Oh, no! No more of your brilliant plans." Stevie's tone was emphatic. "I only end up more deeply involved than when we started." Her eyes grew gentle. "Quintin, let's just give it a rest. I'll make sure I'm not around when Robbie comes to work. Maybe out of sight, out of mind will work."

He confiscated her glass and set it next to his on the floor. "All right," he conceded to her request, "we'll try it your way and see what happens." His arms slid around her waist, his flesh prickling in excitement as he came into close contact with her silken body.

"As for out of sight and out of mind"—his voice was deep and urgent—"even when you're out of my sight, you're always on my mind and in my heart."

"It's the same for me," she breathed, letting her pelvis burrow a feminine message against him. Her teeth sank a gentle love bite into the sensitive skin of his neck; her tongue made tantalizing forays into his ear.

Quintin could feel the heat rising through his body. His hands slithered over the rounded contours of her hips, fingers drawing intricate patterns on her satiny stomach. "I love you." His mouth played with her lips, kissing and nibbling their sweetness.

With a little sigh Stevie locked her arms around his waist, her hands pressing into his well-muscled buttocks. She had been anticipating and planning this moment all night and all day. Suddenly she felt very sexy and deliciously happy in the knowledge she could arouse her man. Her own body taut with mounting passion, she welcomed the bold thrust of his virility.

It was nearly midnight when her phone rang. Instinctively Stevie knew it was Quintin. "Hello, darling."

"Hmmm. I didn't realize you had ESP," came his rueful quip. "What are you doing?"

"Reading *Variety* in bed, with your bathrobe wrapped around me and pretending it's you."

"I envy that robe." His words were like a groan. "I just wanted to call and kiss you good night."

Stevie gave an appreciative laugh. "You're taking Ma Bell much too literally when she says to reach out and touch someone."

"It's just getting too damn hard not to be with you every night," Quintin announced, sounding quite fierce. "I have a planning-board meeting tomorrow. Will you be home at ten?"

"Yes, but"—her teeth gnawed her lower lip— "won't stopping here keep you too late to see Rob?"

"These meetings are nothing I haven't been to before, and my son is too old to be tucked in at night," he jumped in on the defensive. "Besides, I need to see you every day."

"I'll be waiting. I love you, Quintin."

"I love you too."

* * *

"Good heavens, what happened?" Stevie viewed Quintin's stooped posture with alarm.

"I was surveying the site for that clinic this afternoon and fell into a small sinkhole." His hand massaged his back. "I must have pulled a muscle." A wry grin twisted his lips. "It wasn't this bad until I spent two hours sitting at the board meeting in a metal folding chair."

"Listen, why don't you go stretch out on the bed; I've got some liniment that my doctor gave me." She nudged him toward her bedroom. "The stuff smells terrible, but it works like a miracle."

Quintin shivered as Stevie coated his back and shoulders with the icy salve, but almost immediately, under the warming influence of her massaging hands, a deep heat radiated into his muscles. He sighed in relief and nuzzled his face into the bed pillow. "I don't know if it's that awful stuff or if I just feel better because I'm here with you."

She leaned close to his ear. "Compliments will get you everywhere." Stevie shifted into a more comfortable cross-legged position next to him. "Then the clinic is now your baby?"

"Yup. We'll be pouring concrete the first of March," he reported. "Hmmm . . . right there . . . oh . . ."

Her capable fingers kneaded the bunched tendons, and after a few minutes Stevie could feel them begin to relax and stretch into their normal shape. "Sounds as though you're going to be very busy."

"I hope so," he concurred. "I'm putting in a bid on that new county office building that's going up downtown." Quintin turned his head. "How was your day?"

Stevie's palms pushed into his shoulders, making ever-widening circles across his broad back. "Gloria's got the flu and the temporary secretary is . . . let's just say, leaves a lot to be desired. More than one phone call gets him frazzled."

"Him? Wait a minute." He came up on his elbows. "Are you telling me you have a male secretary?"

"I was lucky to get any type of replacement secretary." She pressed him back into the mattress. "It seems all of Nashville is suffering from the flu, and the agency was swamped with requests.

"Chuck's skills aren't too bad. He types eighty words a minute and takes dictation at one hundred ten. Or so he keeps telling me." Stevie blew back a lock of hair that fell across her eyes. "The problem is he can do all that in a school environment, but in an office where nine and ten things go off at once—well . . ."

"Huh," Quintin grumbled, "what's he look like?"

She smothered a laugh. "I can't even remember. Honest." She pressed a kiss to his earlobe. "I like you a little jealous."

He grunted again. "I hope Gloria gets better fast."

"That makes two of us," she breathed. "Whew."

Stevie's head reeled back, the menthol and euca-
lyptus vapors stinging her eyes. "Boy, do you
smell!"

"I guess you'll just have to shower me off,"
Quintin said happily, sitting up and flexing his
shoulders. His dark eyes held hers. "A nurse's
primary responsibility is to make sure her patient is
in perfect working order."

One tawny brow made an elegant arc. "So this is
to be a purely medicinal trip under the shower
massager?"

"Purely," came his stoic answer.

"Come along then, Mr. Ward." Stevie pulled the
strawberry lounge robe over her head and tossed it
on the rocking chair. "I can see my virtue has
nothing to fear," she added dryly and grinned as
she heard his quick intake of breath over her nude
rear view.

Closing the butterfly-etched doors, she inspected
his body with professional disinterest. "Hmmm. I'll
just aim the massage spray on your back," Stevie
said briskly, and turned Quintin around, ignoring
his uncompromising maleness.

Warm needles of pulsating water throbbed
against his shoulders and back. Quintin gave a
contented sigh when once again Stevie's hand
provided an additional rubdown with liquid soap.
The fragrant suds dissolved the biting smell of the
healing liniment, making him feel clean and ap-
proachable.

"Perhaps the patient should give the nurse a
massage," he drawled lazily, shifting positions in

the cubicle. Quintin twirled Stevie around and adjusted the stationary nozzle so the spray hit her shoulders.

"Hmmm . . . that does feel good," she agreed, palms flat against the oatmeal tiled wall. Stevie sighed under the loving assault of masculine hands that ignored her back to concentrate instead on her front.

Blinking the water from her dark lashes, she became hypnotized watching his actions. Creamy soap spilled around gentle, calloused fingers that wreathed her breasts with bubbling lather. She moaned softly, feeling light-headed and intoxicated under his sensual touch.

Quintin moved close behind her, his hands stroking her sleek, pliant form. Fingers meandered across her stomach, taunting the sensitive skin along her inner thigh. His lips worshiped her nape with kisses, his tongue lapping at the dribble of water that slid down her spine.

"Quintin . . ." She turned toward him, wrapping her arms tightly around his neck. "Please . . ." She was shocked to hear herself beg for him.

"Please . . . what?" he rasped thickly.

"Love me." Stevie shuddered at the slow merging of beholder and beheld. Each sought completion in the other and found gratification in that special twilight land that was their unique shared universe.

His arms imprisoned her still-trembling form. "I love you."

She rested against him, feeling at once exhausted

and satiated, the shower now raining a cool spray over their heated flesh. "Quintin . . ."

"Hmmm?"

"I get the impression your back is all better."

"Good afternoon, may I help you?"

Stevie scrutinized the petite, very attractive blue-eyed blonde who was standing at the file cabinet. "I was wondering if I could see Mr. Ward? I'm afraid I don't have an appointment."

"Your name?"

"Stephanie Brandt."

"One moment, please." The young woman crossed to her desk and lifted the telephone, her natural drawl lilting into the mouthpiece of the receiver. "Excuse me, Quintin, there's a Stephanie Brandt here to see you. Quintin? Mr. Ward?"

The bright blue inner-office door was pulled open. "Stevie! What a pleasant surprise! Come on in. Terri, hold any calls." Quintin's knee propelled the door shut; his arms were busy sliding around a slender waist. "What are you doing here?"

Her palms pressed a warm path up his blue-striped shirt, her fingers tracing the Windsor knot on his navy tie. "I had an appointment canceled and a free hour on my hands before my next; I remembered I had never been to your office. So here I am. Glad to see me?" Stevie's eyelashes made a coquettish flutter.

His mouth pressed a silent but unequivocal answer to hers. "I was going to call you about dinner tonight," Quintin said after a long, highly satisfactory kiss. "Thought you might like a more friendly encounter at Le Châlet than our first."

"Oh, I'd love it, but—"

"—you have another engagement," he finished for her. "Some very old client, I trust?"

"A minister and a gospel group."

"Thanks." Quintin grinned. "I can relax knowing your virtue is in absolutely no peril."

"And what about yours?" She gave a quick comeback. "Your secretary is very attractive."

"Her husband thinks so."

Stevie gave an exaggerated sigh of relief. "Are you going to show me around?" She tossed her fur coat on a side chair.

"While Ward Construction does not appear to be as elegant as Brandt Associates"—Quintin gestured around the office—"modesty precludes my dazzling you with a disgustingly healthy profit statement."

Her eyes shifted from his smiling features to the room. It suited him, Stevie decided. Rough-hewn, light gray barn-board panels provided vertical interest in contrast to the three stucco walls; line drawings and black-and-white lithographs were handsome decorator touches. Quintin's desk was a free-form design in black. The leather sofa and accent chairs were also black. Underfoot, white carpeting dappled with black and gray added softness, as did the matching draperies.

Another interior door led into an unoccupied drafting room and a library filled with manuals, grid specs, and mathematical books with titles that

Stevie couldn't pronounce. "If the battery industry ever goes under, I won't be able to add one and one," she told Quintin, her hand lifting a weighty volume entitled *Analytical Trigonometry.* "It's nice to know I'll have you around to handle all of that."

"One of these days do you think we could add one and one and get three?" A possessive hand was placed on her flat stomach. "I can think of nothing nicer than having a little red-haired daughter playing with dolls in Cedar Hill."

Stevie smiled at him, her hand caressing his lean cheek. "I'd love such a merger," came her whispered answer. "We might even add up to four. Five, with Rob."

The silence was deafening as they wandered back to Quintin's office. "I have a hunch your main reason for coming here is that it's three o'clock on Wednesday and Rob is walking into your office right about now," he said not unkindly, settling next to Stevie on the sofa.

"You're too astute," she admitted, resting her head in the comfortable curve of his shoulder. "I've been avoiding Rob. Haven't set eyes on him all week. Has he said anything?"

Quintin's fingers toyed with buttons on the front of her mushroom-colored dress. "Rob seems to be very busy with his studies right now and . . . oh, hell. I've been avoiding him, myself, Stevie," he finally admitted, his voice self-condemning. "I lack the courage to face my own son."

"We've really made a mess of things, haven't we?" she whispered, a lump forming in her throat.

"I just wonder how this will all end." Her bleak gaze meshed with Quintin's.

"I'm praying that your theory of out of sight, out of mind works."

"That makes two of us."

Stevie made sure her appointments outside the office ran late on Thursday. When she unlocked the side door of her office, she found a bouquet of red roses on her desk—Robbie's trademark. She punched the office intercom. "Chuck, who left the flowers?"

"Miss Brandt!" A high-pitched masculine voice registered surprise. "I didn't know you were back. I was just leaving."

"Who left the roses?" Stevie repeated more firmly, shuffling through the conglomeration of papers, calculator tapes, cassettes and assorted office atrocities that littered her normally neat desk. "I can't seem to find a card."

"One of the go-fers," he babbled. "Everything is in such disorder. I don't remember a card. The boy said something about missing you. I don't know. The phone hasn't stopped ringing all day; one of the girls in accounting sneezed all over me when she brought in those files you requested, and I—"

"Go home, Chuck. Forget everything and go home." Stevie collapsed in her chair, staring at the perfect buds that stood silently in a crystal prison but screamed loudly of a problem that had yet to be resolved.

A shaky hand again groped for the telephone.

She called Quintin's home, deciding that if his son answered, she'd simply hang up. But it was Quintin's familiar voice that sent a greeting across the line. "What's the matter, honey? I can tell something's wrong."

"Is . . . is Rob there?"

"He's upstairs, doing his homework."

Stevie took a deep breath. "Quintin, I'm staring at a vase of red roses. A damn baker's dozen sitting smack center on my desk. And I haven't even seen him all week." Her voice was shrill and sniffly.

"Damn! I . . . I . . ." He took a deep breath. "I wasn't going to tell you this, but, well, Rob's all excited; on Friday he gets his class ring."

"Oh, Quintin!" She swallowed the nausea that burned in her throat. "What if he . . . ?"

"Tries to give you the ring?"

"I can't take it. Oh, God, there's no telling what's going to happen."

"Let me come over and we can talk—"

"No." Stevie interrupted. "I . . . I just need some time alone. As a matter of fact, I have to go to a video taping tonight." She was surprised at how easily the lie came. "I'm not sure when I'll be home."

9

~~~~~~~~~~~~~~~~

Wrapped in the security of her mother's teal blue satin robe and warmed by a snifter of her father's best cognac, Stevie was never more aware of the special bond between parent and child. There in their penthouse apartment, with Nashville glittering like millions of diamonds strewn on midnight velvet, she felt their presence and hoped their wisdom would be hers.

Her thoughts centered first on Quintin. His rugged face was indelibly etched in her mind. The thick brown-black hair, the high, intelligent forehead, those melting brown eyes, the tough, sun-weathered skin and the firm, sensuous mouth.

She knew every inch of his body. Her hands, lips and tongue had discovered and explored all the erotic little folds and hollows that made him so much a man. A shiver of pure physical awareness coursed down her spine, but Stevie defiantly shook it off.

Her love for Quintin was more than physical. Their relationship was made up of solid bricks of caring and sharing, trust and fidelity. Stevie felt no need to hang back to avoid career competition because he was secure in his own talents.

But there was an incompleteness about her life that made her sad. While their intimate rendezvous had been thrilling, Stevie wanted to legitimize her love, and she knew Quintin craved that too. Without the firm sense of commitment that marriage involved, she felt uncertain and unsatisfied.

She wanted more than the stolen moments of today, more than memories of yesterday; Stevie wanted the fulfillment of tomorrow. She yearned to call Cedar Hill home and eventually to fill the restored southern mansion with the laughter of children.

Children. Closing her eyes, Stevie pictured Rob. He might be seventeen and on the threshold of manhood, but he was still a child—Quintin's child, and that made him very special.

A reminiscent smile curved Stevie's mouth. The teen-age years were such a vulnerable time of life. The pressures of school were compounded by the pressures of the peer group. Parents were always saying "You're too young" or "You're old enough to know better."

Bodies were changing both on the outside and

the inside, and so were the emotions. How delicate was the balance in their lives.

Unintentionally and through no fault of her own, Stevie had disrupted this delicate balance in Robert Ward's life. All her efforts to discourage Rob's affection for her had only served to strengthen his adolescent love.

The roses and the threat of a class ring hung over her head like the fabled sword of Damocles. Rob was serious in his feelings and Stevie knew just how fragile and tenuous youthful emotions could be.

Stevie drained the last of the cognac from the balloon snifter and placed the empty glass on the oak end table. Despite the softness of the sofa cushions beneath and the downy comfort of her grandmother's quilt on top, Stevie knew she was between a rock and a hard place.

Caught between father and son, no matter what she decided, everyone was going to be hurt. There were degrees of hurt, her mind rationalized, and some could take more pain than others.

If she slept, she wasn't conscious of the fact. Her body may have been resting, but her mind seemed to have been exhaustingly active, and a decision still eluded her.

The morning sun was busily burning off the night, turning the eastern sky into amethyst. Stevie felt in need of a companion. She craved Quintin but turned instead to the television, letting the congenial hosts of the network morning news program assuage her desire.

"The teen-age years are so dramatic," a serious-looking child psychologist stated, "things build up in a child's mind and are blown all out of proportion, and that's when tragedy strikes."

Stevie listened to the man's every word. "There has been an enormous rise in teen and preteen suicides. The children don't seem to find security in their family situations. They feel lost, hopeless and depressed. Too often parents feel their children are just going through a stage, and in some cases this is so.

"I would suggest that if your preteen or teen-ager gets moody or melancholy and becomes antisocial, you first consult a physician for a complete medical checkup. If there is no organic problem, then he should be seen by a psychiatrist, psychologist or counselor.

"Teachers can be helpful by reporting to parents any 'loner' behavior in the child. An extremely introverted child needs help, is actually screaming for help. And let me assure your audience that hundreds of children, some as young as eight and nine, do succeed in taking their lives every year."

The female talk show host shook her head in amazement. "Thank you, Doctor. In a moment we are going to be talking to representatives of Child Find in New Paltz, New York. Child Find is helping to locate the hundreds of thousands of children missing in America. Some are stolen by parents, but the majority are runaways or have just vanished. We'll have an eight-hundred number for you and show you some photos of missing children ranging in age from just a few months old to the late teens. Tomorrow we'll take a look at the growing number of cults that are attracting our youngsters. Right now it's seven-thirty and here's a message from one of our sponsors."

Stevie's shaky fingers reached out to turn off the set. *Suicide, runaways, cults.* Those three words echoed louder and louder in her mind. She knew what her decision had to be. And she realized that she was going to have to be stronger today than she had ever been in her whole life. She couldn't tell Quintin—not just yet. She had to play for time.

She found solace in work. She stayed in her parents' apartment, keeping in constant touch with her office by phone. Most of her time was spent calming and soothing her temporary secretary's high-strung nerves and adding up all the urgent messages Quintin had left both at her office and on her answering machine at home.

It was nearly six on Friday when she returned to Brandt Associates and found Chuck Lewis, the replacement secretary, in the midst of an anxiety attack.

"Miss Brandt, I am so glad to see you." His angular face was nearly lost behind heavy black-framed glasses that succeeded in making his blond hair look bleached out. "There are stacks of messages on your desk from Quintin Ward." A shudder ran through Chuck. "He's a most disagreeable man. Wouldn't believe you hadn't been here all day and threatened me with all sorts of bodily horrors if I didn't tell him where he could find you. Of course I ignored him."

A smile curved her lips. "That's just part of Quintin's charm." She winced as she surveyed Gloria's usually orderly domain. Folders protruded from closed file drawers; the Out basket was overflowing; the In basket was empty; tapes and records were piled in haphazard clumps everywhere. "I see you've been busy, Chuck."

"I've been running myself ragged all day," he grumbled. "Over half of your employees are out with the flu; we're down a mail boy; nothing comes in or out unless I go downstairs and get it or take it down myself." He pointed to a teetering stack of outgoing mail. "I'll drop these on my way home." Sucking in his cheeks, Chuck nodded toward the wall clock.

"Thank you, and I see it's time to leave. I just came in to collect some papers I'm taking to the coast tomorrow." Stevie extended her hand. "Chuck, again, thank you for all your efforts this week. I really appreciate it." Her hand was given a damp, limp shake.

"That's quite all right, Miss Brandt. But please, don't ever request me." He slipped a suede topcoat over his leather jacket. "I'm just not cut out to handle such a rambunctious office."

Her own desk, Stevie discovered, was in worse condition than it had been the night before. It looked as if a bomb had exploded in both offices, leaving a chaos of papers in its wake. She was filling her briefcase with the necessary business papers when the telephone jangled to life. She knew it was Quintin.

She took a deep breath and lifted the receiver. "Hello."

"Stevie! Finally. I've been half out of my mind trying to find you. Worrying about you. Stay right there, I'm coming over. I—"

"Quintin, please, wait just a minute. Hear me out."

The only sound in her ear was his ragged breathing. "For the first time in my life I'm afraid to listen to you."

Emotions threatened to strangle her, but Stevie knew what she had to do and had to say. While the strength of her convictions was absolute, she also knew she didn't possess the courage for a face-to-face confrontation. "Quintin, I love you very much, and nothing and no one else will ever change that."

"All I'm hearing is the word but. Damn it, Stevie, I want to see you, hold you, love you."

"No!" The word was torn from her heart. "Listen to me, please. I've done a lot of thinking about you and me and Rob. Your son is so important to both of us, too precious to hurt in any way." A strange chill enveloped her, making her body quake inside the fur coat.

"What . . . what are you trying to say?" The ache in Quintin's voice echoed her own.

"I'm worried about what might happen to Rob if he ever finds out about us. He's at such a fragile stage in his life right now. His self-esteem and emotional health are too vital and crucial to be damaged in any way."

Bleak eyes stared at the vase of roses; the ruby

blossoms had already begun to darken, their regal heads wilting. "I don't think we should see each other again." Stevie stumbled into her desk chair. Actually saying those words out loud struck a blow that left her crippled.

"Dear God, you can't mean that."

"Please, this is so hard for me." Tears were flowing freely down her cheeks. "I'm very afraid of what Rob might do. He's young and impressionable and . . . and everything is so . . . so life-and-death for him." Stevie wiped her face on the back of her hands.

"I . . . I've made sure that I kept out of his way this week, and I've decided to stay in California for a while." She swallowed hard. "If I'm not around, if Rob can't see me, then maybe all this will pass."

"Let me see you," Quintin begged. "Stevie, I need to see you. I need—"

"No!" Her voice grew stronger. "No, I really feel this is best for both of us." Every fiber of her being screamed a denial. Stevie wanted nothing more than to see Quintin again, hold him, touch him just one last time, but she realized the pain would be too great.

"This is crazy. I'm coming to your office."

"I won't be here and I'm not going home either."

"Damn it, Stevie, you're ruining our lives. You're—"

"I'm trying to save your son's," she cried. "And . . . and my own sanity. I hate the way we've had to keep us a secret. Always looking over our shoulders, wondering if one of Rob's friends will see us. Our love is too beautiful to be sullied any longer by stolen kisses, stolen hours, stolen moments. I want a full, complete life with you, Quintin. I'm proud of you, I'm proud of us. It may be terribly old-fashioned, but I want a wedding ring and to live happily ever after and . . . and I want your babies."

"Love, don't you think I want all those things too?" The anguish evident in Quintin's voice only made Stevie cry harder.

She took a deep breath. "Right now our wants and needs are not as important as your son's. Rob is all that matters." Her tone was soft. "Think of all the years you've already lost with him, Quintin; look how fast he's growing. We can't take the chance of losing him now.

"Rob thinks he's in love with me, and we both know how powerful an emotion love is. What if he discovered that the woman he loves is having an affair with his own father? What do you think that will do to Rob?"

"Don't you dare call what we have an *affair*," Quintin rallied hoarsely.

"It's not to us," Stevie returned quickly, "but it will look like that to Rob. He'll be angry and hurting and he'll want to strike back—get even—and you'll be his target, Quintin. This could kill the both of you."

"Stevie, I don't want to lose you."

Her hand tightened on the receiver. "You'll

never lose me, Quintin," came her whispered vow. "You'll never lose my love. Right now, right this instant, what we have together will only cause pain and suffering. Love shouldn't do that."

"I love you, Stephanie Brandt."

"And I love you, Quintin Ward." Unable to listen to his voice any longer, Stevie slid the receiver back on the phone. She rested her auburn head on the desk as her body was racked with uncontrollable sobs.

The telltale buzzing that signified a dead line finally made an impression on Quintin's mind. A shaking hand hung up the receiver and then moved wearily over his face, fingers mopping the tears that streaked his cheeks.

All that Quintin had feared for his son—anguish, heartache and pain—was now his. His head told him that Stevie was right: Rob must be his primary focus, and he had to be there for his son. But it was Quintin's heart that was bleeding, and the only person who had the power to repair it had just walked out of his life.

"Gloria, how are you feeling?"

"Almost perfect, boss." There was a moment's hesitation on the telephone line. "You don't sound so good, Stevie. Is it the flu?".

Stevie tried to cover the thickness in her voice. "You guessed it," came her lie. "That, and it's been a very long week." A shrill laugh escaped her. "Wait until you see the office. The secretary I got just wasn't up to handling the lunacy that pervades around here."

"Hmmm. Sounds like I have my work cut out for me on Monday," Gloria returned. "Are you all set for your trip?"

"That's one reason I called." Stevie tried to sound casual. "I'll be staying in LA for a while. I'll let you know where later, but I don't want you to give that information out. Not to anyone."

Gloria cleared her throat. "Not even Papa Ward?"

"Not even Quintin."

"Things are that bad? I thought for sure your not seeing Bobby would solve the problem."

"So did I. But yesterday I found a bouquet of red roses on my desk, and Quintin said Rob's all excited about getting his class ring, and—"

"Oh, God. Stevie, do you want to come to my place? We can talk, have a cup of tea—"

She sniffed. "I don't think tea and sympathy are going to do any good. No, Gloria, Quintin and I are just going to have to let each other go."

"I'm so sorry."

Stevie's voice was desolate. "Sorrow is the word. I'll be in touch." She caught sight of her image in the mirror over her mother's bedroom dresser. Her reflection made her flinch. The past few days had taken their toll on Stevie. Her face looked haggard, her hair was dull and lifeless and her eyes were sunk into shadowed hollows.

She had consumed a year's supply of aspirin

trying to ease a perpetual headache, and her stomach was so knotted that it refused any type of food, allowing only tea and water.

While her outer self echoed her inner torment, Stevie embraced the knowledge that ultimately she had spared Quintin's son this same hurt.

10

~~~~~~~~~~

Good morning, Dad. Was that you prowling around the house again last night?"

Quintin carried his coffee cup to the table. "Sorry, son." He gave Rob a halfhearted smile. "I didn't mean to keep you awake."

Robbie poured his third bowl of high-protein cereal, dribbled honey over the multigrain nuggets and added a splash of milk. "Is there trouble at work?"

"No."

"Maybe you're getting the flu," came Rob's prediction.

"Yeah, maybe I am." Quintin's fingers tried to massage the pinching tightness from his temples.

"Well, you're in good company," Rob continued, tapping the Saturday morning paper. "The virus made the front page. Half our school is out too."

Quintin stirred sugar and milk into his coffee. "How are you feeling?"

"Fine. It's all the vitamins, Dad." Rob nodded toward the collection of plastic bottles that dominated the top of the refrigerator. "You should really try them. It's the natural way to keep your body and your mind healthy."

Stevie does that for me, Quintin mused, *or did.* He sighed again. "Anything new at school? We haven't had much of a chance to talk this past week."

"I know how busy you are, Dad. I respect your dedication." His jaw moved steadily, molars trying to pulverize the cereal. "Everything's first-rate. I'm really into cameras. Tommie's 3-D is incredible. The two of us have joined the photo club and we're learning how to develop our own stuff, use lights and shadows. Would you mind if I borrowed your thirty-five millimeter?"

"No. No, go ahead. It's in the closet in my den."

Robbie took a mouthful of orange juice. "Say, Dad"—he swallowed hard, hesitating slightly—"there's no school next Friday. Do you think I could have a party? Invite some of the guys and their dates over. I'd help Mrs. Crawford with the eats and the cleanup."

The coffee hit the back of Quintin's throat and made him gag. "A party? Well . . . huh . . . I suppose so. Huh . . . who'd be your date?" He almost dreaded to ask the question for fear of hearing Stevie's name.

"Tommie."

Quintin's jaw dropped. Had his son gone to another extreme? "Huh, Rob"—a shaky laugh escaped him—"a *Tommie* is not what I had in mind for my son's date."

Rob's brown eyes blinked in momentary confusion. "What? Oh, for gosh sakes, Dad." His lips split into a broad grin. "Tommie's a girl. I . . . I mean, a woman." A musical sigh was emitted.

Quintin ran a hand through his hair. "I thought Stephanie Brandt was the woman in your life."

"She's last year, Dad." He spread butter on a slice of whole-wheat toast. "I don't even work there anymore."

"You . . . you what?" Quintin's voice rang in disbelief.

"I went over after school on Tuesday and told them I was quitting." Rob folded half the bread into his mouth. "The photo club meets two of the days I was scheduled to work. But don't worry"—he held up his palm—"I've got a new job that starts next week. Tuesday, Friday and Saturday afternoons at the Yogurt Junction in the mall."

"Rob, you want to run all this by me again?" Quintin folded his hands quietly on top of the table. "Three weeks ago you were threatening to run away if I interfered with your seeing Stevie. Two weeks ago she was the most wonderful thing that ever happened to you. You had never been happier in your whole life. And now . . . now . . ." Words failed him.

"Three weeks is a whole lifetime, Dad," Rob returned seriously. "Besides, Tommie only moved here ten days ago. It was instant karma between us," he recounted in a dreamy voice. "She's beautiful. Five foot two, sky-blue eyes, long blond hair that she wears in one of those French braids. Tommie's a brain. Honor Society. She wants to be a vet. She also makes the most delicious bean sprout sandwiches."

"I . . . I see," Quintin mumbled, although he wasn't quite sure he did.

"You're going to love her, and her folks are okay. Maybe we could have them over for dinner sometime?" Robbie inquired. "Tommie's mother is crazy over antiques, and she was all excited about seeing what we've done to Cedar Hill."

Quintin nodded mutely.

"You'll like Mr. Hammond—that's Tommie's dad," he continued. "He's in advertising and marketing. You should see all the crazy commercials he's got on video tape. Better than any TV show."

"Where . . . where does Stephanie Brandt fit in all this?" Quintin finally mustered the courage to ask.

"I don't understand."

"Didn't you just send her a bouquet of red roses?"

Rob bristled. "Hey, if that florist sent you a bill, it's a lie. If I wanted to give flowers to anyone, it'd be to Tommie. But she only likes plants. She's into living flora and fauna."

"Then Stevie is no longer the great love of your life?"

"Well, she's okay." Robbie shrugged. "But she doesn't look at life the way Tommie does. Tommie sees and breathes the energy being transmitted around her. She's electric." Another sigh escaped him. "The last week and a half with her has been greater than the sum total of my life. She's everything. Tommie's the ultimate."

Quintin scrutinized that familiar dreamy look on his son's face. "That's just what you said about Stevie," he persisted.

"Stevie was fine for a while," Robbie admitted, returning to earth to reach for more toast. "She's just . . . just . . ." He fumbled for the right word. ". . . too old." He licked the butter off his fingers.

"And she's the worst date I've ever had. Do you know she scraped the sprouts off her salad and drowned the tofu in oil and vinegar?" His narrow shoulders shuddered beneath his school insignia sweatshirt. "She's a washout at the video arcade, and when we went to the basketball game, she kept getting her raccoon tails caught in the hinges of the bleachers."

His father smothered a laugh. "Must have been very embarrassing for you."

"For sure." Robbie nodded. "Stevie's just going to have to realize she's not young," he continued, his voice serious. "I don't think she can handle the excitement of being with someone my age." His fingers curled around an apple in the fruit basket on the table. "Stevie would do better with someone . . . your age, Dad. Someone who's . . . you know, not as active."

Quintin's hand reached out to halt the apple's progress into his son's mouth. "Let me ask you a hypothetical question." He smiled. "Would it upset you to know that Stevie started going out with someone else?"

"No."

"How about if she and this other man fell in love and wanted to get married?"

"Fine with me." Robbie transferred the Delicious apple into his other hand and lifted it to his anxious mouth. White teeth splintered the red skin and sank into the smooth white fruit.

"How about kids? Would you mind if they had kids?"

"More power to them."

Quintin cleared his throat. "Just one more question: What would you say if . . . if I was that man?" He held his breath and braced his emotions.

Robbie chewed for a full minute while he considered the idea. "You might give it a try. Do you really think she's your type? I mean, she's too tall, and I don't think she owns a pair of jeans."

"I'll take my chances."

"Say, if Stevie was to be my stepmother"— Rob's brown eyes widened—"I bet she could get the Pit Stops to perform at the senior ball. That would be a knockout!"

Sagging against the back of the captain's chair,

Quintin felt at once exhausted and energized. Suddenly he became a mass of moving arms and legs. He had to find Stevie and tell her that everything was all right. Everything was better than all right: It was wonderful!

Quintin lifted the receiver, then slammed it down. He hadn't any idea where to get in touch with her. The office was closed on Saturday, her damn answering machine was useless, and . . . he snapped his fingers under a surge of inspiration.

"Rob"—he fought to sound calm—"are you going to be busy this weekend?"

"Tommie and I are taking our cameras downtown to shoot a photo journal on the contrasting images in Nashville. It's for extra credit in civics."

"Would you be upset if I left Mrs. Crawford in charge and went to California? I'd be back on Tuesday," he promised.

"Of course not, Dad." Robbie shrugged. "I'll probably end up eating over at the Hammonds' anyway. Tommie's mother wants me to bring over my yogurt culture; she just bought a maker."

"Thanks, Rob." Quintin put his arms around his son and gave him a grateful hug. "You don't know how much this little talk has meant to me."

After quickly filling in his housekeeper, Quintin drove the fifteen miles to the airport in seventeen minutes. It would have been faster, but the trooper who issued him a speeding ticket on Interstate 40 wasn't the least bit interested in aiding Cupid.

His tennis shoes ate up the airport hallways as he systematically checked all fourteen airlines that served the terminal. Quintin didn't know what company Stevie was flying—he didn't even know what time her plane left—but he staunchly refused to acknowledge the fact that he could have missed her. Fate wouldn't be that cruel.

Approaching the ninth reservations-and-information counter, his dark gaze locked onto the familiar feminine form that had alternately pleasured and tortured his days and nights. Even though her back was to him, Quintin knew it was Stevie. The platinum-toned blouse and slacks fit her tall, lithe body to perfection.

His hand settled against the slope of her waist at the same instant that his chin balanced on her shoulder. "Hello, darling."

Stevie's startled squeak turned quickly to a gasp of pleasure, then just as suddenly into a cry of distress. "Quintin!" Her fingers gripped his muscled forearm. "What are you doing here? Oh, God, Rob didn't find out? He hasn't done anything stupid; he's all right, isn't he?" She hastily began blinking back tears that stung her eyes.

"He's fine. Everything is fine. I came to be with you." His knuckles caressed the hollow beneath her cheekbone. "I love you."

"Quintin, please." She stared at him, her eyes devouring every rugged feature. "What's happened? I'm so confused."

His hand pressed against her lips. "We straightened out everything over breakfast." A grin suddenly lightened his expression. "You've been replaced," he announced, "by a girl named Tommie who has a 3-D camera and makes sprout sandwiches."

"What!" Stevie lowered her voice, noting the interested stares of the other people who were in line. "When did all this happen?"

"Last week," he told her, "while we were happening, they were happening."

Stevie took her position at the airline counter, handing the reservations clerk her ticket. "What about the roses," she demanded, "and all that talk about the school ring?"

Quintin's broad shoulders lifted in a perplexed shrug. "I have a hunch Tommie's getting the ring. Rob said the flowers weren't from him." He aimed a sly smile at her. "Are you holding out on me? Is there someone else?"

"I'm not going to dignify that question with a response," came her regal intonation. Stevie scratched the back of her head. "With Gloria out and the office in such a mess"—she sighed—"I guess a client could have sent the roses. I never did find a card, and I just gave up sorting through all the phone messages."

The uniformed airline attendant slid Stevie's boarding pass into the ticket folder. "You're all set, Miss Brandt. Better hurry, Flight Three Ninety-Eight is just about ready to board at Gate Two."

"We'll have another one of those," Quintin interjected, fumbling in the back pocket of his jeans for his wallet. He slapped the two halves of his

American Express card on the counter. "I'm coming with you."

The clerk eyed first the broken card and then the man. Her professional gaze swept over his navy velour sweatshirt, well-worn denims and in-vogue sneakers. "Do you have any luggage?" At his negative response her brow lifted. "I'll have to call and verify this number. One moment, please."

"Tell me more about Rob." Stevie pestered him for further information while they waited. "I want all the details."

Quintin leaned his elbow on the counter, watching with approval as the color seeped back into Stevie's complexion. "Well, there's just no way to break this to you gently, love." His tone was laced with laughter. "You're too tall and too old, and you just can't keep up with a young, active person."

"Well"—her lips formed a pout—"I like that!"

A deep chuckle rumbled in his chest. "I know I do!" Quintin chucked her under the chin. "It appears as though my plan did do its job," came his smug retort. "Rob said you're a drag as a date, don't appreciate health food and are no good at Pac-Man, and it seems he was quite embarrassed at that basketball game by the way you were dressed."

"Of all the nerve," she sputtered.

"Excuse me, sir." The reservationist pushed a credit slip and a pen toward him. "Sign right there and"—she handed him a red-and-blue-striped packet—"here's your ticket. Gate Two, and please hurry."

Hand in hand, laughing like children, they ran for the plane. The doors on the wide-bodied L10-11 were locked into place as they clicked on their seat belts.

"I just can't believe you're here." Stevie's hand slid inside Quintin's, her fingers coupling intimately with his. "I was so miserable, and now . . ." She breathed a contented sigh, her auburn head snuggling into the curve of his neck.

Quintin lifted her hand to his lips and pressed a kiss to her ring finger. "When we get to California, the first thing on our agenda is a ring. I want everyone to know that you're taken." His tone was quite fierce.

"Suits me," she whispered. Her tongue drew a teasing heart on the sensitive skin below his ear. "I love you."

"I'd like to love you," came his low growl. "Do you know how long it's been?"

"Eighty-one hours, twelve minutes and"—Stevie twisted his arm to view his watch—"four seconds. But, Quintin"—her lashes fluttered provocatively—"I don't think the people on this airplane would appreciate your jumping my body in first class."

"Champagne?" a pert blond stewardess inquired.

"Yes," came their united approval.

"Did you two just get married?" She smiled and handed them each a glass.

"Not yet." Stevie smiled back.

"We're just on the honeymoon," came Quintin's dry undertone.

"You made her blush," Stevie hissed.

"I'd rather make you blush," he countered, fidgeting despite the oversize seat. "How much of this trip is business?"

"As of right now, just tomorrow night's American Music Award." She clicked her glass with his. "The rest of the time we'll practice for our honeymoon." Suddenly Stevie turned serious. "Quintin?"

His hand molded her cheek. "Shhh . . . I don't want to see that scared look in your eyes," Quintin warned. "Everything is fine. Rob's parting comment was that when you do become his stepmother, he wants the Pit Stops for the senior ball."

"I'm glad." Her shoulders relaxed into the cushions. "But I would like Rob to help us plan our wedding—make suggestions—for the three of us to become a family."

Quintin leaned over her, his mouth brushing against hers. An urgent groan rumbled in his throat. "I wish we were on a train; at least they have bunks."

"Behave yourself." She pushed at him. "You know you still have to pass my father's inspection." Her tawny brows lifted in silent warning.

"Approved or not, lady," Quintin growled,

"nothing or nobody is going to keep us apart"—his hand slapped the armrest—"unless it's this airplane."

An announcement was made that the in-flight movie was about to start. "Here." Stevie handed him a set of earphones from the pocket of the seat. "The movie will keep your mind off your glands." One hazel eye favored him with a saucy wink. "These James Bond epics are filled with gadgetry, stunts, explosions . . ."

"And half-naked girls," Quintin finished.

"I thought it was *my* body you craved," she said haughtily.

"It is." He turned his head, panting noisily at her.

"Stop it." Stevie plugged the earphone jack into the socket. "Now what's the matter?" she asked as he unhooked his seat belt.

"I don't think the champagne settled right." His hand moved to rub his stomach. "I'll be fine." Quintin ambled down the wide aisle, ignoring the first-class lavatories to inspect the tourists in the tail of the plane.

Adjusting the audio knob for the earphones, Stevie settled in to watch the movie. Five minutes later the stewardess nudged her arm and handed her a note. Frowning, she unfolded the paper and squinted at the scrawled message: First bathroom on the right—Q.

Unhooking her seat belt, Stevie made her way through the darkened plane. Her knuckles rapped lightly on the lavatory door; she hoped he wasn't too airsick.

The door opened an inch; brown eyes inspected the caller, and a familiar hand snaked out to pull her roughly inside. "What—?"

"Shhh." Quintin pressed his finger against her lips as he threw the bolt that locked the door and marked it Occupied.

"Are you all right?" Stevie peered at him. "Are you sick?"

"Nope." His arms slid around her waist, pulling her tightly against him. "I'm very, very healthy." Quintin's hips rubbed suggestively into hers. "See?"

"Yes. I do." Her hands splayed on his broad chest. "Quintin, you are very naughty."

"Why, because I want to be alone with the woman I love? Can't I just hold you for a while?" His lips roamed over her neck, along her chin. "I love you."

She rubbed her cheek against his. "I feel so happy, so complete." Stevie pulled her head back slightly. "From now on we start all our days together."

"And end them the same way," Quintin promised. His lips caressed her mouth, his tongue making a languid advancement into the honeyed sweetness. His hands pulled her blouse free of the waistband of her slacks to slide warmly over her spine; arrogant masculine fingers released the hooks on her bra.

"What are you doing?" Stevie hissed.

"I love you too much, lady."

She melted under the exquisite torment of his mouth and hands. "Quintin, you can't do *that* on an airplane."

"Who says?"

"The FAA or the FCC or the FBI. I'm sure some government agency with initials frowns on this." She could feel the hungry urgency that tensed his body begin to claim her own. The need to consummate their love was suddenly quite fierce and uncontrollable. "We're probably going to get into trouble," she whispered, helping him off with his shirt.

"Do you really care?"

Hazel eyes locked into brown. "Right at this moment, not one iota." Her fingers luxuriated in the virile curls that covered his sinewy torso. She pressed quick, hard kisses over his chest and shoulders. "Do you know how much I love you?"

"Yes, I think I do." Quintin easily dispensed with the buttons on her blouse; his fingers freed her breasts from their loosened lacy cradles. He bent his head, his mouth homing in on her taut nipples. A satisfied sound announced his pleasure as he tasted the velvety swells.

Her body was drowning under waves of delicious sensations. She could feel him harden beneath her caressing hands; her fingers sought the zipper of his jeans as he unbuttoned her trousers.

With a low groan of aching desire, Quintin merged their bodies into one perfect unit. "Till death do us part," came his husky pledge, his voice reflecting the depth of his emotions.

"And beyond," she whispered. Stevie wrapped her arms tightly around his neck, savoring the feel of him inside her. "Quintin, I knew you could make the earth move, but the heavens too . . . ?"

Genuine Silhouette sterling silver bookmark for only $15.95!

What a beautiful way to hold your place in your current romance! This genuine sterling silver bookmark, with the distinctive Silhouette symbol in elegant black, measures 1½" long and 1" wide. It makes a beautiful gift for yourself, and for every romantic you know! And, at only $15.95 each, including all postage and handling charges, you'll want to order several now, while supplies last.

Send your name and address with check or money order for $15.95 per bookmark ordered to
Simon & Schuster Enterprises
120 Brighton Rd., P.O. Box 5020
Clifton, N.J. 07012
Attn: Bookmark

Bookmarks can be ordered pre-paid only. No charges will be accepted. Please allow 4-6 weeks for delivery.

N.Y. State Residents
Please Add Sales Tax

YOU'LL BE SWEPT AWAY WITH SILHOUETTE DESIRE

$1.75 each

1 ☐ James
2 ☐ Monet
3 ☐ Clay
4 ☐ Carey

5 ☐ Baker
6 ☐ Mallory
7 ☐ St. Claire

8 ☐ Dee
9 ☐ Simms
10 ☐ Smith

$1.95 each

11 ☐ James
12 ☐ Palmer
13 ☐ Wallace
14 ☐ Valley
15 ☐ Vernon
16 ☐ Major
17 ☐ Simms
18 ☐ Ross
19 ☐ James
20 ☐ Allison
21 ☐ Baker
22 ☐ Durant
23 ☐ Sunshine
24 ☐ Baxter
25 ☐ James
26 ☐ Palmer
27 ☐ Conrad
28 ☐ Lovan

29 ☐ Michelle
30 ☐ Lind
31 ☐ James
32 ☐ Clay
33 ☐ Powers
34 ☐ Milan
35 ☐ Major
36 ☐ Summers
37 ☐ James
38 ☐ Douglass
39 ☐ Monet
40 ☐ Mallory
41 ☐ St. Claire
42 ☐ Stewart
43 ☐ Simms
44 ☐ West
45 ☐ Clay
46 ☐ Chance

47 ☐ Michelle
48 ☐ Powers
49 ☐ James
50 ☐ Palmer
51 ☐ Lind
52 ☐ Morgan
53 ☐ Joyce
54 ☐ Fulford
55 ☐ James
56 ☐ Douglass
57 ☐ Michelle
58 ☐ Mallory
59 ☐ Powers
60 ☐ Dennis
61 ☐ Simms
62 ☐ Monet
63 ☐ Dee
64 ☐ Milan

65 ☐ Allison
66 ☐ Langtry
67 ☐ James
68 ☐ Browning
69 ☐ Carey
70 ☐ Victor
71 ☐ Joyce
72 ☐ Hart
73 ☐ St. Clair
74 ☐ Douglass
75 ☐ McKenna
76 ☐ Michelle
77 ☐ Lowell
78 ☐ Barber
79 ☐ Simms
80 ☐ Palmer
81 ☐ Kennedy
82 ☐ Clay

YOU'LL BE SWEPT AWAY WITH SILHOUETTE DESIRE

$1.95 each

83 ☐ Chance	90 ☐ Roszel	97 ☐ James	104 ☐Chase
84 ☐ Powers	91 ☐ Browning	98 ☐ Joyce	105 ☐Blair
85 ☐ James	92 ☐ Carey	99 ☐ Major	106 ☐Michelle
86 ☐ Malek	93 ☐ Berk	100 ☐ Howard	107 ☐Chance
87 ☐ Michelle	94 ☐ Robbins	101 ☐ Morgan	108 ☐Gladstone
88 ☐ Trevor	95 ☐ Summers	102 ☐ Palmer	
89 ☐ Ross	96 ☐ Milan	103 ☐ James	

READERS' COMMENTS ON SILHOUETTE DESIRES

"Thank you for Silhouette Desires. They are the best thing that has happened to the bookshelves in a long time."

—V.W.*, Knoxville, TN

"Silhouette Desires—wonderful, fantastic—the best romance around."

—H.T.*, Margate, N.J.

"As a writer as well as a reader of romantic fiction, I found DESIREs most refreshingly realistic—and definitely as magical as the love captured on their pages."

—C.M.*, Silver Lake, N.Y.

*names available on request